THE VERY BEST IN BRITISH MYSTERY—
PRAISE FOR HAZEL HOLT'S
MRS. MALORY MYSTERY SERIES

"Holt's sleuth remains as charming and politely inquisitive as ever." —*Publisher's Weekly*

"Anglophiles will delight in the authentically British Mrs. Malory, and mystery fans will enjoy Holt's stylish writing, dry wit, and clever plot."
—*Booklist*

"A delectable treat for cozy-lovers, British style."
—*Kirkus Reviews*

"If you haven't discovered Mrs. Malory, I highly recommend reading the rest of the series."
—*Mystery News*

"A charming slice of British village life."
—*Chicago Sun Times*

"A British whodunit that works a traditional mode to good effect . . . delightful."
—*Cleveland Plain-Dealer*

"Irresistible." —*Yakima Herald-Republic*

"A soothing, gentle treat. . . . The literate, enjoyable Mrs. Sheila Malory is back." —*Atlanta Journal*

MRS. MALORY: DEATH AMONG FRIENDS

A Sheila Malory Mystery

Hazel Holt

A SIGNET BOOK

SIGNET
Published by New American Library, a division of
Penguin Putnam Inc., 375 Hudson Street,
New York, New York 10014, U.S.A.
Penguin Books Ltd, 27 Wrights Lane,
London W8 5TZ, England
Penguin Books Australia Ltd,
Ringwood, Victoria, Australia
Penguin Books Canada Ltd, 10 Alcorn Avenue,
Toronto, Ontario, Canada M4V 3B2
Penguin Books (N.Z.) Ltd, 182–190 Wairau Road,
Auckland 10, New Zealand

Penguin Books Ltd, Registered Offices:
Harmondsworth, Middlesex, England

First published by Signet, an imprint of New American Library, a division of
Penguin Putnam Inc.

First Printing, June, 1999
10 9 8 7 6 5 4 3 2 1

Printed in the United States of America

for Flip
and in loving memory of Phi
but for whom this book
would have been written in half the time

Chapter One

"Oh Lord!" Rosemary groaned, indicating a sheet of paper sellotaped to the tiles above the sink. "She's at it again!"

I leaned forward to read the notice.

> Will the person who removed the rubber gloves from this draining board please return them at once. They are my personal property and are expensive to replace.
>
> Signed Freda Spencer
> Chairman, Management Committee

The job of Chairman of the Management Committee of Brunswick Lodge is usually considered to be the sort of thankless task that no one in their right mind would want to be lumbered with. Rosemary and I both agree that the fact that Freda Spencer actively sought the position, indeed seems to revel in it, says a great deal about her character.

Brunswick Lodge, a handsome Georgian building, although owned by the local council, is leased at a peppercorn rent to the Friends, who run it as a sort of up-market community centre, with concerts, play-readings, and such mild cultural activities as Taviscombe is prepared to accept. It is also a popular venue for jumble and bring-and-buy sales and there is a sort of permanent exhibition of pictures and artefacts relating to Old Taviscombe in what is grandly, if erroneously known as the Museum Room. There is a non-resident caretaker, Mr. Soames, an unhelpful man who is supposed to keep the place clean, but doesn't, and the house is generally maintained by volunteers.

As anyone who has ever tried to run *anything* with the help of volunteers will know, it is not easy. A very high standard of tact and diplomacy, if not downright sycophancy, is essential if personalities are not to clash and umbrage is not to be taken. Unfortunately, Freda Spencer, though possessed of many other qualities necessary for a successful leader (perseverance, determination, and downright bossiness) is palpably lacking in the gentler arts and, since her elevation to the

Chair, has managed to alienate a fair number of useful helpers.

"Oh dear," Rosemary said, "I wish she wouldn't! There'll be nobody left at all if she goes on like this! Poor Lilian Baker was almost in tears because Freda was so beastly to her when she forgot to turn the lights out in the Committee Room and they were left on all night—a mistake anyone could make. And Jack says that Maureen Philips is thinking of resigning from the committee because of the way Freda rides rough-shod over everyone's suggestions."

Rosemary's husband, Jack, is also on the Committee and, being a man who has no inhibitions about expressing himself forcefully, has had some notable battles with Freda.

"I know," I agreed. "It is difficult. But she *does* get things done, you must admit—remember how rundown everything was before she took over?"

"Yes, I know all that, but Freda really is the limit!"

"Oh, I agree, she's the end! But, honestly, who on earth would take on the job if she didn't do it?"

There being no reply to this, Rosemary remained silent.

"And really," I continued, "her energy's quite

remarkable, considering she must be in her late seventies by now. I just wish I had half her vitality!"

"Just think," Rosemary said, "what she must have been like in the war."

Freda Spencer, as she never tires of telling anyone who will listen, had been an officer in the WRNS. Her brisk manner certainly brings with it more than a hint of the quarterdeck and her conversation is still sprinkled with service slang. It is obvious that she has every intention of running Brunswick Lodge as a tight ship.

"Well, you know people are so vague and woolly-minded," I said, "they really do sometimes need a bomb behind them to get things done."

"I can't think why you're defending her," Rosemary protested, "when you know you can't stand the woman."

The sound of the kitchen door opening made us both swing round guiltily. But it was only Sybil Jacobs, who loathes Freda even more than we do.

"Hello, what's this then?" she said, coming over to the sink. "Yet another of Freda's notices? Oh, I think that was me. I used them when I washed up after the coffee morning on Wednesday. I put them away in this drawer, here." She opened the drawer by the sink and took out a pair of yellow rubber gloves and laid them with some solemnity on the draining board. "There. Now perhaps her ladyship will be satisfied. Honestly! what a fuss about nothing. Typical of Freda!"

Rosemary sighed. "Talking about a fuss about nothing, Jack says she was banging on about having tighter security everywhere—locks on windows, special fastenings on doors, that sort of thing. It'll cost a fortune! Derek Forster told her the money simply wasn't available, but she wouldn't listen, you know how she is. She just tanked over him and now *he's* offended and we'll never get another treasurer half as good."

"It's absolutely ridiculous!" Sybil said roundly. "Apart from a bit of petty cash there's nothing worth stealing here, anyway. Unless"—her voice took on a satirical tone—"Freda thinks that the objects in the Museum Room might attract the attention of a gang of international art thieves!"

"I suppose," Rosemary said, "she was thinking of vandals breaking in and doing a lot of damage. There was that business down by the sea front . . ."

"A few yobbos who've had too much to drink breaking up a bus shelter isn't the same thing at all," Sybil protested. "Anyway, there are perfectly good folding, wooden shutters on the downstairs windows."

"I know. But you know what Freda's like once she's got her teeth into something—she's not going to let up. She'll make everyone's life a misery until she gets her own way."

"Oh well," I said resignedly, "we'll just have to see. Now then, could you both very kindly give me a hand to lug this box of books upstairs?"

Rosemary and I were in Brunswick Lodge making preparations for the Christmas Fayre held every first Saturday in December since time immemorial. Rosemary had the produce stall and I (because of my vague connection with literature) was in charge of the book stall.

"Oh, just a minute," Sybil said to Rosemary. "I must just hand over this jam and lemon curd." She started to unload a quantity of jars from her shopping basket onto the worktop.

"Oh, lovely!" I said. "I adore lemon curd and it's so tedious to make—all that stirring in double saucepans! It's very popular, it goes in a flash. I must make sure I get in early."

"Take a jar now," Sybil said.

"No, I mustn't," I protested. "I'm always complaining about the way helpers grab the best things for themselves before the public get a look in."

"Oh, don't be silly! Here—if it makes your conscience feel any better, take this jar as a personal present from me to you and then you can make a suitable contribution to funds in general. How's that?"

"A very persuasive piece of sophistry." I laughed, taking the jar and putting it in my bag. "Thank you very much."

Rosemary, who had been turning over some of the books in the box, held up a couple of depressing-looking volumes. "*Electrical Wiring for Beginners* and a life of Annie Besant! Who on earth will buy those?"

"You never know," I said. "Some young couple doing up their first home who just happen to be theosophists . . ."

"Why do we never get some rare first edition?" Rosemary asked. "Or even," she continued more practically, "some decent detective paperbacks?"

"There's a lovely big pile of Mills and Boon," I said, rummaging about in the box. "They always go well. And several cookery books."

"Oh, let me look," Sybil said. "No, that's no good—Indian and Mexican. Pauline would never eat anything like that. Her idea of adventurous eating is a Spanish omelette!"

Pauline is Sybil's twin sister. Since they were both widowed they now share a house, and, although they are really devoted to each other, they seem obliged to take up diametrically opposite views on absolutely everything. Rosemary says it's the only way they can assert their individuality, which is probably true, but it's very wearing for all their friends.

"I'll never forget how absolutely maddening she was in Rome that time," Sybil went on. "I could scarcely get her out of that English tea-room by the Spanish Steps. And asking for thinly-sliced bread and butter, if you please, when we were in Doney's in Florence!"

Although they are now both well into their seventies, Sybil and Pauline are still keen travellers, bickering their way around the globe with great enthusiasm. Not only to the usual tourist places, but also to less frequented bits of the Middle and even the Far East where thin bread and butter is, I imagine, quite unobtainable.

"Where are you going next year?" I asked.

"We thought Calabria. Start at the bottom and work upwards to Naples. I'd like to see Naples again. I was there in the war—it's probably quite spoilt now. Funnily enough, Freda was in Naples too, a lot of Wrens were, but not at the same time as me, thank God! At least, I never ran across her."

"I didn't know you were in the Wrens, Sybil," I said.

"No, Pauline and I were nurses, Queen Alexandra's, quite the best thing to be in. You got sent absolutely everywhere."

"Were you together all the time, you and Pauline?" Rosemary asked.

"At first we were. We joined the FANYs at the beginning of the war. God! That was a wonderfully crazy set-up in those days. I once found myself driving an Admiral of the Fleet in full dress uniform across Salisbury Plain in a racing car in a snow storm—but that's a long story. Then after a bit we transferred to the QA's and Pauline went to India and I went to South Africa—Simonstown—and then Gibraltar, and ended up in Naples. That's where I met Maurice."

"Fantastic," Rosemary said. "England must have seemed pretty tame after that."

"Well, I wasn't here all that long. Maurice was in the Foreign Office, so we moved about quite a bit. But when he died and Pauline was on her own too, we somehow both drifted back to Taviscombe. You know how it is."

"It's funny, really," I said, "how many people *have* come back. There's you and Pauline. And Freda, too, for that matter. And Leslie and Jean Evans and Matthew and Elizabeth Fenchurch and Richard Lewis—oh, heaps of people!"

"All coming back to their roots," Rosemary said. "I suppose it's something you do when you're getting older. It's nice for us old stick-in-the-muds who never left the place. Makes us feel we made the right choice after all!"

"Well, quite a lot of people who went away will be coming back in January," I remarked. "The school reunion, remember?"

"Goodness, yes," Rosemary said. "I must send in our form for the dinner. Let's all try and sit together. Last time Jack and I were stuck at a table with Alan Watson and that awful wife of his. *He* gave us a ball-by-ball description of every game of golf he's ever played and she went on and on about this apartment they have in Spain. Jack was barely civil by the end of the evening."

"Oh yes, please, I'd like that," I said gratefully. As a female on my own I have been landed only too often with uncongenial dinner companions.

"You can count us in too," Sybil said. "But won't Jack mind being the only man surrounded by four females?"

"He'd enjoy it," Rosemary laughed. "But I suppose I could ask Richard Lewis to even things up a bit. He's not exactly a sparkling conversationalist but he's a nice old thing."

"Oh, I expect *he'll* want to be sitting with Freda," Sybil said. "He's always hanging round her."

"That's true, he really is devoted."

"Has been for years," Sybil agreed. "I think Freda found him quite useful when she first came back to Taviscombe, after Bill retired. And of course she used him as a sort of unpaid nursemaid for Bill when he had that second stroke, and then when *he* died Richard was handy to do things around the house and take her out to dinner. Poor sap!" She sniffed derisively. "But his nose must be right out of joint now."

"You mean Laurence?" Rosemary asked.

Instinctively, we all drew closer together and lowered our voices. Laurence Marvell was Freda's new constant companion. As far as we could judge, he was in his mid-forties, very good-looking with thick dark hair and a tall, elegant figure, impeccably dressed in a rather theatrical way (double-breasted waistcoat, velvet collar on his coat), and with the most charming manners. All this would have been unusual enough in this day and age, but what marked him out in Taviscombe (conservative in every sense of the word) was that he made no secret of the fact that he was gay. Although he frequently referred to his friend Jimmy, it looked as if that relationship was now in the past and he seemed to have no present attachment. Unless you counted his continual dancing attendance on Freda.

"Of course, she *pays* for everything," Rosemary

said. "When they go anywhere—out to dinner or the theatre in London or that trip to Paris for lunch, on the Shuttle. I suppose that's the attraction."

"She certainly seems besotted," I said. "It was Larry this and Larry that the last time I saw her."

"It's disgusting!" Sybil said gruffly. "Surely she must see that she's making a fool of herself and people are laughing at her behind her back."

"It would never occur to Freda that anyone would *dare* to laugh at her, even behind her back," I said.

"Well, they do," Sybil persisted. "Even Olive was talking about it the other day, and you know how loyal she usually is."

Olive is Freda's cousin. They were more or less brought up together, although Olive remained in Taviscombe, looking after her father when her mother died quite young. Of course they kept in touch and then when Freda came back here she co-opted Olive as a sort of lady-in-waiting. Olive, being quite different from her cousin, meekly acquiesced and was usually to be found one step behind Freda on most occasions. The fact that Olive had actually voiced concern showed how far things must have gone.

"He really is wonderfully civil," Rosemary said

dreamily. "Exquisitely polite, lovely old-fashioned manners one had thought were gone forever."

"Oh, yes," I agreed. "I can quite see how anyone could be bewitched—it's just the fact that it's Freda that makes it so remarkable."

"Where did he spring from, anyway?" Sybil demanded.

"I think he was a schoolmaster somewhere in London," I said. "I don't know where. Freda told me he took early retirement on health grounds."

"He looks healthy enough to me," Sybil snorted, "and I wonder who pays for his clothes. You can't tell me a retired schoolmaster could afford that overcoat; it's Aquascutum. I saw the label when he took it off at the concert last week."

"Yes," Rosemary agreed, "and that was a Ralph Lauren polo shirt he was wearing the other day. I saw the little logo thing."

"Perhaps Freda bought them for him," I suggested. "She's pretty comfortably off."

"In that case," Sybil demanded, "why doesn't she do more for that wretched daughter of hers?"

Freda's only child, Emily, had made an unwise marriage against her mother's wishes. She was a very pretty girl, with Freda's dark, curly hair, great brown eyes, and slim figure, and it was fairly obvious that Freda (who was a bit of a snob) had hoped for some sort of grand alliance, or at least a marriage into one of the professions. Instead, when Emily was at Cambridge she had fallen in love with another student, Ben Merrick—not the scion of a noble house with endless acres, but the son of a toolmaker in the Midlands, with no money and no prospects. Freda had forbidden the match but, in the first and most devastating rebellious act of her life, Emily had married Ben anyway. He had ideas about self-sufficiency and ecological correctness and they had ended up on a tiny smallholding in Devon, which Emily bought with a legacy from her father. I think they were happy together but, with very little money, it was a distinctly Spartan existence. Freda had very publicly declared her intention of washing her hands of the whole affair and the phrase "made her own bed and now she must lie on it" was bandied about from time to time whenever Freda remembered past injustices she deemed had been done to her.

Olive, who had never married, had always been very fond of Emily and had, she once confided in me, been surreptitiously sending what money she could to support the young couple, who had compounded their imprudence in Freda's eyes by having three children very close together.

"You'd think, wouldn't you," Rosemary said,

"that Freda would have some sort of feeling for her grandchildren? I don't think she's ever *seen* them."

To Rosemary, who dotes on and is deeply involved with her own two grandchildren, this is quite the most incomprehensible part of the whole affair.

"She probably doesn't want dear Laurence to think of her as a grandmother," Sybil said sardonically. "She's always buzzing about like a two-year-old!"

"Well, as we were saying before," I said, "she really is amazing for her age. She's still remarkably handsome."

And she is. Tall and upright, with her dark hair only lightly (and attractively) streaked with grey, and, since she has that pale, very thick skin that never seems to show the wrinkles, she doesn't look anything like her age. She spends a lot on clothes, too, and is a constant (and favoured) customer of Taviscombe's only fashionable dress shop, Estelle's, as well as getting a lot of her things in Bath and Exeter or even London. In fact, it is the times when Freda sends in some of her cast-offs for a jumble sale that the helpers really do descend like locusts to have the first pick before the public can get at them.

"Handsome is as handsome does!" Sybil has

never hesitated to express her feelings by means of a cliché. "She's far too full of herself and I, for one, look forward to the day when someone takes her down a peg. Pride," she added, with the air of one making an original statement, "goes before a fall."

Chapter Two

As it happened, I had an opportunity to observe Freda and Laurence Marvell together the very next day. I'd had a tiresome morning trailing around Taviscombe trying to find some braid for a rather nice Victorian dining chair I was attempting to re-cover. The shops in Taviscombe are not what they were. Now the place is full of tourists; when each shop falls empty it's promptly converted into yet another place to sell postcards, "novelties," or cheap clothing, so that it's almost impossible to find such necessities of life as braid, narrow elastic and tea-strainers. I felt tired and irritable and not at all like making lunch for myself, so I parked the car by the harbour and went into the pub down there for a restorative gin and tonic and a sandwich.

On a late November day it was empty of the noisy crowds that would throng the bar later in the season. In fact, I was the only customer and able to choose a table as far away as possible from the flashing (though mercifully silent) pinball machines. I'd just settled down and was opening my copy of the *Spectator* to have a nice peaceful read, when I saw that two other people had come into the bar and one of them was greeting me.

"Sheila! Lovely to see you! Do you mind if we join you?"

It was Laurence. Freda, who was with him, seemed less delighted to see me but she sat down at my table with at least a semblance of good humour. It occurred to me that Laurence must, by now, be finding Freda rather exhausting, and had seized the opportunity to dilute her company.

"There now," Laurence said, "isn't this cosy. Your usual vodka and tonic, Freddie? How about you, Sheila, are you ready for another one?"

"No, thanks," I said, "I'm fine."

"Right. What about food? I think you'd like the pasta special, don't you?"

To one who knew only too well the old despotic Freda, this calm assumption of authority was a revelation. Freda, however, when he went up to the bar to order the food and drink, merely said smugly, "Larry always knows what I like."

It was the same all through lunch. Laurence led

the conversation, while Freda either murmured confirmation of his views or drew my attention to what she obviously considered his wit and intelligence, rather like a proud parent showing off a beloved child. For his part, Laurence treated her with a mixture of masterfulness and flattery that she obviously found irresistible.

"Now then," he said, "what about a pudding? Sheila, you *must* have something delicious after that austere sandwich. They do a very good sticky toffee pudding—that's what Freddie and I are going to have. Do join us."

"I'd love to," I replied, "but I daren't. I'm trying to lose a bit of weight before the excesses of Christmas."

"Oh, I know! It's dreadful, isn't it? Just a few calories extra and I blow up like a balloon—not like tiresome Freddie here, who eats like a horse but still manages to keep that fabulous figure." Freda practically bridled with pleasure. "Still," he continued, "I'm going to throw caution to the *winds* and so must you. Think how *awful* I'd feel tucking in with you looking all smug and puritanical!"

"Oh, all right," I said, laughing. "You win!"

"Good girl!" He gave me a conspiratorial smile. "We poor, weak-willed souls must stick together!"

Freda smiled indulgently. "That's absolute nonsense. Larry keeps very fit. He goes to the gym almost every day and swimming, too, twice a week."

"The gym?" I enquired.

"Up at the Westwood Hotel," she replied. "There's a private health club there now. I'm a member, too. You ought to join, Sheila." She looked at me critically. "You look as if you could do with getting into shape."

"Oh, I always mean to take more exercise," I said, "but I never seem to have the time. Anyway, walking the dogs is quite strenuous."

"Nonsense!" The old forthright Freda was back. "At our age one needs a regular programme of exercise to stay really fit."

I opened my mouth to protest that Freda was the best part of twenty years older than me, but there seemed little point.

"You should see Freddie," Laurence said, "tearing up and down the pool doing her Australian crawl. Just like an Olympic champion!"

Freda looked complacent.

"I quite like swimming," I said, "but not a gym. All that terrifying equipment would put me off."

"But that's just what you need to tone up the muscles," Freda declared. "So important! I spend half an hour a day on my exercise bicycle at home."

"Goodness!" I said.

"And Larry and I go jogging most mornings."

"How splendid!"

"I'll get them to send you an application form for the health club," Freda said. "It's quite expensive, but that's quite a good thing because it keeps out the riffraff."

I murmured something that might be construed as thanks and addressed my pudding.

Noting my lack of enthusiasm, Laurence tactfully changed the subject. "We're going up to London next week," he said, "to see that new thing at the Royal Court."

"Yes," Freda broke in, "a friend of Larry's has got the leading part in it."

"Really?"

"Yes," Laurence said. "Tim Daniels. Do you know his work?"

"Oh, yes. I know. I haven't seen him in the theatre, but I remember him in that hospital series on television."

"Larry knows him quite well," Freda said proudly, as if knowing a moderately successful television actor conferred some sort of special status. "So we're going backstage afterwards."

"How lovely. Do you know many actors?" I asked Laurence.

"A few. You know how it is. My friend Jimmy is in the theatre so I ran into people at first night parties and so on."

"I wonder if you've come across my friend David Beaumont?"

"Oh yes, of course I know Dave. Lovely chap, absolutely charming."

Since, to my certain knowledge (going back over forty years), no one has ever called David "Dave," I found my mistrust of Laurence Marvell growing.

"I tell Larry *he* should have gone on the stage," Freda said. "With that marvellous voice."

Certainly he had a good voice, deep and resonant.

Laurence laughed. "I did a bit at university. But I was never brave enough to go into the profession—I could see too many of my friends spending too much time resting. No, schoolmastering seemed a safer option!"

"Where was your school?" I asked.

"It's a prep school—Bennett's. You may have heard of it."

"I think I have—it's in Kensington, isn't it?"

"A *very* good school," Freda broke in. "Some very influential parents!"

"But you retired early?" I asked.

"Yes, my wretched asthma," he said. "I was advised to move out of London to the sea."

"Did you know anyone in Taviscombe?"

"No, but I've always loved the place, ever since I used to come here for holidays with my parents."

"Are your parents still alive?" I felt I was cross-questioning him rather obviously, but I was very curious about his background and it seemed too good an opportunity to miss.

"No, alas," he said sadly, "they are both dead. I have no family—well, only one elderly aunt."

"The poor lamb's an orphan," Freda said, laying her hand on his arm.

He turned and gave her a warm, intimate smile. "An orphan I may be," he said, "but with *such* good friends."

As she smiled back at him, I could see that Freda was totally infatuated and I wondered just where that infatuation might lead her.

"Quite besotted," I said to Rosemary when she came round to have coffee and borrow my icing set. "She obviously dotes. And really I wouldn't trust him as far as I could throw him! Dave, indeed! He's obviously doing everything he possibly can to impress Freda."

"I'm surprised Freda is impressed with all this theatre stuff," Rosemary said.

"Oh, it's the culture bit," I replied. "You know she's got this *thing* about never having been to university because of the war, so she's extra keen on the Arts to show just how cultured she really is."

"Extraordinary! But you're right, of course. Chairman of the Music Society and Secretary of the Arts Society and she's always read *all* the novels short-listed for the Booker, however unintelligible! It's sad, really."

"Well, Laurence Marvell is certainly playing on all that," I said. "He's buttering her up like mad."

"Oh well." Rosemary put down her coffee cup. "I suppose if she wants a toy-boy at her age, that's up to her."

"Hardly a toy-boy!" I said. "He's a bit old for that. In a way this is more dangerous. He's really taken over her life."

"And I suppose you can see the attraction," Rosemary said thoughtfully. "It's given her a tremendous fillip. I mean, there she was, all set in her ways, bossing people about at Brunswick Lodge, going on as she always had, tanking over everyone. It must have given her a bit of a thrill to have someone come over all masterful."

"She certainly did seem to be enjoying it," I admitted.

"And he's very personable, tall and good looking, a charming accessory!"

"More than that, I think. He really seems to have a hold over her; it's almost a complete personality change. The old Freda flashes out every so often—she was her offensive self about my need to get into shape, as she calls it. She was going on about the new health club they both go to."

"The one at the Westwood?" Rosemary asked. "Well, far be it for me to agree with anything Freda says, but *I've* been thinking of joining, for the swimming. Actually, why don't we both join? It might be fun. You know we used to love the old Lido."

The Lido, an outside swimming pool with a café attached, had been very much part of our youth, a social meeting place for the young of Taviscombe, where the girls in their shirred cotton swimsuits sat at tables round the pool, self-consciously drinking milk-shakes and pretending to ignore the boys who were lounging about on the diving boards trying to look like Johnny Weismuller.

"Goodness, yes, the Lido! How glamorous we

all thought it was. The water and the tiles both that particularly *brilliant* shade of turquoise."

"Do you remember Ian Sully?" Rosemary asked. "And how gorgeous we thought he was? And he was only interested in Denise Westcott, especially when she got that two-piece swim-suit—that *was* a sensation! Mother nearly had a fit when she heard about it. She said the whole family were immoral and wouldn't let me go to tea with Denise's sister Margaret, which was unfair on Margaret, who was dull as ditchwater, so I was quite glad of an excuse to get out of going."

"Oh yes, and Richard Lewis—he seemed so grown-up and splendid—well, he was, of course, he'd been a pilot in the war and everything—and he was very goodlooking in those days. I can remember him standing on that top diving-board looking absolutely *stunning*. Lois Montgomery had a terrific thing about him, always following him about and hanging around outside his house hoping for a glimpse."

Rosemary sighed. "Heigh-ho! The days of our youth!"

"Well," I said, "we'll be able to relive it all—good and bad—at the reunion."

We were silent for a moment and then Rosemary said, "What about joining this health club?"

"Oh, all right, I will if you will. But *after* Christmas. I really haven't a moment between now and then to *breathe,* even. I've got a few Christmas cards but no presents at all and Anthea said that it's absolute hell trying to find anywhere to park in Taunton *already.*"

"God, yes! And I'd better go back and get on with my Christmas cake. Though why I bother, I don't know. Nobody ever eats the damned thing, they're all too full up with turkey and pudding, so it hangs around in its tin until March, looking reproachful."

"I'm not making one this year," I said. "Michael doesn't like it and Hilda can't eat it because of her peculiar digestion, and I certainly can't get through a whole one on my own."

"Hilda's definitely coming to you for Christmas, then?"

"Yes." I sighed. I am deeply fond of my cousin Hilda, she is the kindest of mortals, but she is not an easy guest, having firmly-held (and expressed) views on such controversial subjects as food and cooking (mine), friends (Michael's), the Series Three service (the Church of England), and the Welfare State (both the Government *and* the Opposition).

"Bring her for drinks with us on Christmas Eve," Rosemary said.

"Oh, that would be lovely! But you know what she's like."

"You can let her loose on Jack, he likes a good argument. Anyway, if last year's little shindig is anything to go by, there'll be so many people there, all shouting at the tops of their voices, that no one will hear a word she says."

Chapter Three

The day of the Christmas Fayre came and was just as tiring as I knew it would be.

"Goodness, I'm exhausted!" I said as I eased off my shoes and sank into a chair. "Michael, be a dutiful son and pour me a large G and T. It really is dreadful the way good works drive one to hard drink."

Foss, who can never see anyone sitting down without wishing to join them, sprang onto my lap. I took a grateful sip from the glass Michael handed to me and put it safely away on the table beside me. Although Siamese cats prefer sherry, they are not averse to gin and tonic and I didn't want a sharp, seal-pointed face peering hopefully into my glass.

"So. How did it go?" Michael asked.

"Oh, quite well, I think. Derek hadn't added up all the cash when I left, but I should think we made about three hundred pounds, which isn't bad at this time of the year, when there're so many Christmas things that people want to spend their money on."

"I thought the idea was that they'd all buy the ravishing little objects you were selling for Christmas presents."

"That's the theory. But, honestly, who gives lavender bags and woolly bedjackets nowadays? The children's clothes sell well, but it would be a brave parent or grandparent who gave a child a hand-knitted sweater for Christmas rather than a Sonic Hedgehog or whatever it is they have nowadays."

Michael laughed. "Which reminds me, what are you giving me?"

"Wait and see. Actually, I haven't bought you anything at all yet, so I'm entirely open to suggestions, provided it's something I can get locally. I don't think I can *face* Taunton or Exeter."

"Well, I saw a rather nice suede jacket in Hobbs'. It's a bit expensive, but if it would save you a journey . . ."

"Horrible child! Oh, all right. Go and try it on and if you like it I'll give you a cheque."

"Jolly good. Then I can wear it for the Christmas concert."

The Christmas concert was (obviously) an annual event at Brunswick Lodge, consisting of readings with a vaguely Christmas flavour, some carols, and a couple of piano pieces. This year Michael had been asked by Sybil, who organised it, to read the inevitable passage from *A Christmas Carol* that always winds up the occasion.

"If you like. I thought a suit would be nice, though."

"Oh, Ma, you can't expect me to wear a *suit*!"

"All right, all right. It's up to you. I just thought a suit would be more formal and Dickensian. Who else is reading this year?"

"Richard Lewis and Muriel Partridge, as well as Sybil, of course."

"Of course." Sybil was a leading light of the local amateur dramatic society.

"Oh yes, and that man Laurence Marvell is reading a couple of poems."

"Really?"

"Yes, Freda Spencer made Sybil have him. I think she threatened not to play the piano if he wasn't given something, and, although I think Sybil would have loved to say, Well, don't play, then, she didn't quite dare."

"How fascinating! Actually, I should think he'd be quite good. He's got a splendid voice."

"He's not bad—a bit affected, but okay. He's

doing the Betjeman and that Thomas Hardy thing."

"What's Freda playing? Her usual Liszt, I suppose."

Freda is a competent pianist, quite good technically, though her playing always seems to me to be lacking in feeling. She tends towards rather showy pieces full of twiddy bits to show off her expertise.

"I don't know. Something with lots of notes."

"Well," I said, "there's no way we could have a Christmas concert without Freda. It would really be *Hamlet* without the Prince."

"The atmosphere was pretty tense between Sybil and Freda at rehearsal. Well, Freda was her usual self, but Sybil seemed very on edge and snappy with her. *Not* much of the Christmas spirit there!"

"Freda can be a bit much sometimes," I said, heaving myself reluctantly from my chair, "especially if one isn't feeling very strong, and Sybil is involved in so many things just now I expect she's just tired. I thought we'd have spaghetti tonight. I made the sauce yesterday so I've only got to heat it up."

The days sped by, as they always do in December, and, urged on by the relentless countdown

("Only eighteen more shopping days to Christmas!") on the radio and in the newspapers, I seemed to spend more and more of my time darting in and out of shops, making and losing lists and standing in queues in the post office behind elderly ladies who wanted to send registered parcels to Western Australia.

"And of course I've run out of cards," I said to Rosemary when we met in Smiths'. "Every year I make all the usual lists and buy what I think will be the right number and somehow there's always someone I've forgotten or someone not on my list who sends a card out of the blue!"

"One year," Rosemary said, "I'm going to be really strong-minded and *not* send cards to people just because they've sent one to us. Well, that's what I say—but I know perfectly well that when it happens I'll bung one back at them as I always do."

"It's a sort of atavistic instinct," I agreed. "You feel something terrible will happen if you don't."

"It's quite ridiculous, of course," Rosemary went on. "There's the Davenants—we haven't seen them for years, and even when we did I never liked them. Yet year after year we exchange meaningless enquiries about each other's health and insincere wishes about meeting again. Sheer cowardice, that's what it is! We're all caught up in this ludicrous system."

"And now, of course, all the decent cards have gone. Do you think I could get away with these wildlife ones?" I turned over a few cards in the box. "This hedgehog in the snow is quite sweet, though not exactly Christmassy."

"The snow?" Rosemary suggested.

"Heaven forbid!" I exclaimed. "Life is fraught enough as it is without a white Christmas."

"Why don't you see if there are any Brunswick Lodge ones left?" Rosemary suggested.

Maureen Philips is a rather good artist and every year she designs a Christmas card which is sold in aid of Brunswick Lodge funds.

"What a good idea," I said. "It's a rather nice one this year. I'll pop along now and hope there are still some there."

"Freda said they were having some more printed so I expect there will be. Actually, I might come along with you. Jack left his pen there after the committee meeting last night and I'd better go and see if anyone's found it."

At Brunswick Lodge we were surprised to see a police car parked outside and when we opened the main door a young constable was standing in the hall, apparently engaged in a mindless perusal of the ceiling.

"Whatever's happened?" Rosemary asked. "It's Constable Sully, isn't it?"

"Yes, Mrs. Francis."

"So what's happened?"

The young man shifted awkwardly. He had obviously been told to say nothing, but when confronted by his Chief Inspector's mother-in-law (Roger Eliot is married to Rosemary's daughter, Jilly) he clearly didn't know what to do.

"Sergeant Pope's in the office," he suggested hopefully.

"Right." Rosemary moved purposefully towards the office and I followed behind. The constable returned to his contemplation of the ceiling.

The office was in some disarray. Several chairs were overturned and there were papers scattered over the desk and some on the floor. There was also an open cash box on the desk and what looked horribly like a small pool of blood. Sergeant Pope, a stout, comfortable man whom I knew slightly (his wife is a member of the Women's Institute), was over by the window looking at a sheet of paper. Standing by the desk, his hands clutching the back of a chair as if for support, was Laurence Marvell, staring down at the pool of blood as if hypnotised by it.

The sergeant looked up when we came into the room, and quickly turned his initial exclamation of annoyance into a greeting when he saw Rosemary. "Good morning, Mrs. Francis, Mrs. Malory." He acknowledged us with a slight nod of the head. "Nasty business."

"What's happened?" Rosemary asked.

The sergeant shook his head slowly from side to side as if to emphasize the gravity of what he was about to say. "It's Mrs. Spencer," he said. "She's been attacked."

"Freda!" I exclaimed. "Attacked? Not here!"

"I'm afraid so."

"But what happened?"

"Someone hit her over the head and took some cash from this box here and her handbag."

"How is she?" Rosemary asked.

"They've taken her to the hospital." Laurence spoke quietly. "She was unconscious, you see. We haven't had any news yet. I'm going to see her as soon as the sergeant here has finished with me."

"Finished with you?"

"I found her."

"How awful," I said. "It must have been a dreadful shock."

He looked at me gratefully. "Yes, it was. She came in to go through the membership lists, something to do with making a new appeal, and she asked me to pick her up at eleven-thirty. We were going out to lunch at a new place I found at Dunster. I came in and . . ." He broke off.

"Was the front door open?" Rosemary asked.

"Yes."

"Perhaps you could help with this, Mrs. Francis." Sergeant Pope had obviously decided that it was time the questioning was placed on a more formal footing. "Mr. Marvell didn't seem to know if the front door should have been unlocked."

"Well," Rosemary said, "what's today? Tuesday, isn't it? Then there wouldn't have been a steward on duty—we're having an awful job finding enough volunteers, reliable ones, that is—so officially the place should have been closed. But I expect Freda would have thought that as she was here she might as well open up. The office is right next to the front door, so she'd have heard anyone coming in."

"She obviously didn't hear whoever it was today," Sergeant Pope observed drily.

"Goodness, no, she didn't." Rosemary looked confused. "But *usually* . . . I mean, we'd none of us expect anything like *this*!"

"Well," I suggested, "a burglar creeping about,

trying not to make a noise, would be quite different from any ordinary visitor walking about in a normal way."

"Very true, Mrs. Malory." Sergeant Pope gave me a half smile.

"It just shows," I went on, "Freda was right about the security here being useless."

"As you will see," the sergeant pointed to the cash box, "he got away with whatever was in here. Do you have any idea how much that might have been?"

"Not much," Rosemary said, "just the money from the coffee morning yesterday. That's usually about twenty pounds and about ten pounds' petty cash."

"And her handbag, sir." He turned to Laurence. "Would there be much in that?"

"I wouldn't think so. Certainly not more than fifty pounds, though there'd be credit cards and so on." Laurence made a helpless gesture with his hands. "Oh, God! Do you mean that all this was for less than a hundred pounds? That's terrible!"

"It would be terrible," Sergeant Pope said austerely, "however much money was involved."

Laurence looked confused. "Yes, of course, I didn't mean that. It's just . . ."

"Did you say she was hit on the head?" Rosemary asked. "What was she hit with?"

"We're not sure," Sergeant Pope replied. "Probably nothing here—though until the SOCO people have had a look we won't know for certain. But it looks as if he took it away with him, whatever it was."

Rosemary shuddered. "She might have been killed."

Laurence gave a little unsteady laugh. "It would take more than a knock on the head to kill Freda," he said. "But I would feel happier if I could get to the hospital to see her. So," he turned to the sergeant, "if that's all . . . ?"

"I think so, sir." He consulted a notebook. "You arrived here at eleven-twenty and found Mrs. Spencer lying here unconscious, her head on the table. You didn't see anyone leaving or inside the building. You telephoned for an ambulance and for us and awaited our arrival. Yes, thank you, sir. I think that will be all for now. If you'd just write down your name and address here. That's fine. And, after you've been to the hospital, perhaps you'd be good enough to come down to the station and we'll take a formal statement for you to sign. Actually," he shut the notebook and put it in his pocket, "I'll be visiting the hospital shortly myself to see if Mrs. Spencer is fit to make a statement."

"Yes, well," I said, making a move towards the

door, "we'd better go." I turned to Laurence. "Will you give me a ring, when you've been to the hospital, and let me know how she is?"

"Yes, of course."

The three of us walked out into the street together. The sky was dark and overcast and there was a bitter wind that seemed to go right through you.

Laurence turned his coat collar up. "What a horrible day," he said.

I wasn't sure if he was referring to the weather or to the awful thing that had just happened. Perhaps both. He half raised his hand in salute as he turned and went down the road to the hospital.

"I'm terribly afraid it might be going to snow," I said. "We may have a white Christmas after all."

Rosemary shivered. "Have you got to get back for anything?" she asked. "If not, let's go and have lunch at the Buttery. I really don't feel like cooking anything after all that."

"I wondered," Rosemary said as she poked experimentally at the pasty on her plate, "if we should have gone along to the hospital with him?"

"I don't think so," I said. "If she has come round—and pray heaven she has—it'll be Laurence she'll want to see."

"Mm, yes. I've often wondered about that." She cut the pasty open and regarded it suspiciously. "There's an awful lot of potato and carrot in this thing; I can't find the meat. How's your fish pie?"

"Too much potato. This place is really going downhill. I can't think why we still come here."

"Oh, it's convenient, I suppose. But Freda and Laurence Marvell . . ."

"I know, it is odd. I mean, he's never made a secret of the fact that he's gay. But somehow I've never thought of Freda as a—what is it they call it?—a fag-hag. No, I think he's just a charmer on the make and she's fallen for it. And why not, really, if it makes her happy?"

"Olive wouldn't agree with you," Rosemary said. "She's very upset at the way Laurence has sort of taken the place of Emily. You know how fond she is of her and the children."

"I don't think Freda thinks of him as a surrogate son. More of a cicisbeo—is that the word I want?—you know, someone safe who used to escort married ladies in eighteenth-century Italy."

"Well, whatever the relationship is, I think it's a bit peculiar. Jack is very forthright about it, as you can imagine!"

I laughed affectionately. "Dear Jack. Life is always black and white to him. It must simplify matters a lot."

"It does for him," Rosemary said ruefully, "but not necessarily for other people."

I pushed aside the congealed remains of my fish pie. "Do you want a pudding or shall I just get us coffee?"

"Oh, just coffee. This pasty, though disgusting, was very filling."

As I was standing in the queue a voice behind me said, "Hello, can I join you?"

It was Sybil. She sat down at our table and Rosemary told her what had happened.

"Freda! Hit over the head! Good God!"

"We don't know how she is," I said. "She was unconscious when they took her to the hospital."

"It would take more than a knock on the head to finish off Freda."

"That's what Laurence said."

"Laurence?" She looked at us enquiringly.

"He found her," Rosemary explained. "He'd gone to pick her up to take her out to lunch and there she was, lying in a pool of blood."

I shuddered. "It really does make you think. It could have been any of us, on duty on our own! Freda was quite right when she said there ought to be more security."

"Oh, Freda is always right," Sybil said.

There was a bitterness in her tone, over and above the usual acidity that was always there when she spoke of Freda. I looked at her curiously. As with Freda, one always forgets quite how old Sybil is, but today she was looking her age. Even in the fairly dim light of the Buttery one could see that the lines on her face were deeply etched and her eyes, their lids heavily wrinkled, were rimmed with red as old people's are. She looked very tired.

"Still," Rosemary was saying, "we'll have to take extra precautions now, otherwise *nobody* will fancy doing stewarding. Jack's always said that there should always be two people on duty at once, though, even together, old Miss Farjeon and poor old Mr. Whipple wouldn't stand much of a chance against the sort of thing that's happened today."

"We really do need some more young people," Sybil said.

It was understood that by "young" we all meant retired people in their sixties rather than their seventies or eighties. Really young people (even those of us in our fifties counted as young in this context), it was recognised, led lives that were far too busy and didn't have the time to spare for that sort of thing.

"I know," Rosemary agreed. "But where *are* they? People are coming down to Taviscombe to retire all the time, but *we* never seem to get them."

"It is a bit of a facer, though," I said. "Even a couple of years ago this sort of crime would have been unthinkable in a place like Taviscombe, but now—well, we accept it as normal, almost."

"It isn't even," Sybil said, "as if it had happened in the summer when the town is full of all sorts of undesirables. I suppose that means it is one of our local yobs. I don't suppose Freda saw who hit her?"

We both looked at Rosemary as if her connection (albeit by marriage) with the police made her an authority on such a thing.

She shook her head. "No, I'm afraid not."

"Well," Sybil said briskly, "let's hope the police catch whoever it was quickly."

"Sergeant Pope is very good," Rosemary said. "Really reliable—I'm sure he'll know where to look." She got up and reached for her shopping bag under the table. "I'd better go. I've just remembered I said I'd collect Miss Webber's prescription and take it in for her."

"And I must go as well," I said, "in case Laurence tries to phone me with news of Freda. Oh, bother! I wasn't able to look for those Brunswick Lodge Christmas cards, and I don't suppose I'll be able to get in now. Oh well, I'd better go back to Smith's and get those hedgehogs."

Chapter Four

Freda was all right. Indeed, she was well enough to play at the Christmas concert the following week. She was wearing a bandage round her forehead, which gave her the rather dashing appearance of a 1920s lady tennis player.

"Surely," Sybil said sourly, "she can't *still* need a bandage? A small dressing would be perfectly adequate by now."

But the general opinion was that Freda was very brave, indeed noble, to be carrying on in this splendid way.

"If I've said I'll do something," I heard Freda saying to Lilian Baker, "then I will certainly keep my word. I am not the sort of person who makes a habit of letting people down."

"But your poor head!" Lilian protested.

Freda gave her brisk little laugh. "Oh, my skull's like teak! In Plymouth, in the war, we were delivering stores to the ships in the blitz and I got hit over the head by a falling timber when a building collapsed. Right as rain a couple of days after. And that wasn't the worst thing that happened to me by a long way! Young people today make such a fuss about trifles."

Lilian murmured admiringly.

"They should bring back conscription," Freda went on. "That would give these young layabouts a bit of discipline, keep them out of trouble. *That* would cut the crime rate!"

"Such a dreadful thing to have happened," Lilian said.

"Have the police had any luck in finding who did it?" I asked.

Freda gave something like a snort. "Luck! What they need is a little application, a little hard work." She eyed me severely, as if it was somehow my fault that no progress had been made. "They did," she added grudgingly, "find my handbag."

"Really? Where?"

"It had been stuffed into that litter bin across the road. So, of course, I'll never be able to use it again. It was a very good one, too, a very fine, soft leather. I got it at Selfridges the last time I was in London with Larry."

"Was there anything still in it?" I asked.

"Well, yes, as a matter of fact, everything was there—credit cards, keys, everything. Only the money had gone."

"Goodness!" I exclaimed. "Wasn't that fortunate! It would have been a dreadful bore to have had to have all your locks changed and that tiresome bother with the bank about credit cards and things. I remember when I lost my cheque book it was endlessly complicated . . ."

"Yes, I suppose it could have been worse." Freda never wanted to hear about anyone else's experiences. "Nevertheless," she continued triumphantly, "it does serve to emphasize how *right* I was about the security here. I've ordered locks for all the windows and special mortice locks for the doors."

"That will cost a pretty penny," I said. "Can the Trust afford it?"

"Afford it or not," Freda said grandly, "it has to be done. Now I must go and check that my music is in the right order. Last year some fool messed about with it and muddled it up."

She moved over to the piano where I heard her complaining to Derek Forster about the instrument (quite a good one, actually) not having been tuned specially for the occasion.

"Well, you have to hand it to her," Rosemary said, coming up with a sheaf of programmes for us to hand to latecomers, "she really is indomitable."

"I know. Right back to her most irritating form," I replied, "and loving all the attention."

The concert was, as it always is, moving and heart-warming. The readings were splendid (Laurence Marvell read as beautifully as I thought he would) and I glowed with maternal pride at the appreciative murmurs after Michael's reading of Dickens. We all enjoyed singing the carols—always one of the high spots of Christmas for me—and Freda positively galloped through the Schumann and the rather showy piece of Liszt she had chosen.

Afterwards, when people were milling around clutching their glasses of rather too mulled wine, Rosemary and I circulated with plates of mince pies, which had been made with varying degrees of expertise by the usual volunteers.

"Do have a mince pie," I said to Olive Clark. "No, not that one, it's one of Daphne Meadows' heavy-handed wholemeal ones. Have this one here with the lattice top, that's Rosemary's. Did you enjoy the concert?"

"Oh, yes!" Her round, rather sad face broke into smiles. "And dear Michael read so beautifully. You must be very proud of him."

"He was good, wasn't he? Of course, Peter

used to read very well. I suppose he takes after him."

Olive has always had a soft spot for Michael. When he was small she used to take him out for little treats ("Can I borrow that dear child of yours for the afternoon?"); indeed, she loves all children and they invariably like her. Peter used to say that it's because she has a childlike quality herself, a sort of wonder at the world that the young instinctively respond to.

"I love the carols," I said. "It's always nice just to let go and sing without worrying about how your voice sounds. And Freda played very well. We all thought it was splendid of her."

"Freda has always had a gift for music."

"I do hope doing this hasn't set back her recovery. I mean, her head is still bandaged and she must have been dreadfully shaken."

"She was in hospital for several days," Olive said, "because they wanted to keep her under observation. But there was no concussion and the wound was, fortunately, clean."

Her voice was coolly professional and I looked at her enquiringly. She gave me her soft, defensive smile.

"I was a nurse here at Taviscombe Hospital during the war so I do have a little medical knowledge." She sighed. "I wanted to join one of the services, they all sounded so glamorous! But I couldn't leave Papa—my mother died when I was a child, as you know—so it was the only thing I was able to do."

"I never knew that," I said.

"It would have been nice to get away," she said wistfully, "to have gone out into the real world—well, it seemed like the real world at the time—but I knew Papa needed me."

"Duty," I said, "it's almost a forgotten word. The daughter at home."

"Oh, I loved Papa," Olive protested. "I wanted to be with him. It's just that it would have been nice to have seen a little of the world. By the time he died I was too old, too set in my ways, too afraid, perhaps, to strike out on my own." She smiled again. "Goodness me, I *am* going on. You shouldn't be such a good listener, my dear!"

"It's nice to have a chat," I said. "We never seem to catch up on things. Why don't you come to lunch next Sunday? I know Michael would love to see you."

"That would be lovely. I'll look forward to it."

Sybil and I did the washing up and Richard Lewis put away the chairs.

"The same old people doing things as usual," Sybil grumbled. "It really is too bad."

"Oh well," I said charitably, "people are always

busy so near to Christmas. I'm more or less organised now. At least, I think I am, though there's bound to be something vital I've forgotten and only remember after the shops are shut on Christmas Eve. Are you and Pauline going to be at home for Christmas?"

"No fear! We're going to Greece—Kalamata. Marvellous at this time of the year, no tourists, quite empty, absolutely peaceful."

"It sounds lovely," I said, thinking of the hassle with the turkey and making the right sort of stuffing that wouldn't upset Hilda's precarious digestion. To get right away! But I suppose I'm so programmed to the idea of a traditional Christmas that anything else wouldn't seem right! I wrung out the dishcloth and draped it over the washing-up bowl. "I'll put these things away," I said. "You get along."

"Well, I will, if you don't mind. There's a programme I want to listen to on Radio Three. Richard's still here, he'll lock up."

The kitchen at Brunswick Lodge is large and high-ceilinged with a walk-in larder at one end, which is where we keep all the china and glasses. I had just taken the last pile of plates into the larder and had the door half-closed behind me when I heard voices in the kitchen.

"Here," Freda said impatiently, "those chair

cushions go in that cupboard. Surely you know that by now."

"Freda!" Richard Lewis's voice was strained and eager. "I must talk to you."

"I haven't time now."

"Please, Freda. You know how I feel, how I've always felt. And now, when this terrible thing has happened to you . . . Freda, won't you marry me and let me care for you?"

"Oh, for God's sake!"

Greatly embarrassed, I edged behind the larder door, standing very still so that they wouldn't see me.

Richard burst out, "I know—I know you've always refused me before, but I thought that now we're both old it might be different. I love you, you know that. I've loved you for so long now. Even after you married Bill. And then, when he died you seemed to need me and I hoped . . . I just want to look after you."

"I don't need you to look after me." There was a taunting note in Freda's voice. "Larry does that." Something like a low moan came from Richard and she snapped, "For pity's sake, Richard, don't be so wet!"

"Freda, please. You mustn't trust him. He's only after your money, everyone says so."

"You know nothing about the matter! Larry is

devoted to me and I am to him. And I certainly wouldn't marry *you*, Richard, if you were the last man on earth—you're feeble and dreary and the most Godawful bore! Oh, for Christ's sake, man, stop snivelling. If only you knew how ridiculous you look."

"Freda!" His voice broke on a sob.

"I'm not staying here any longer to listen to you whining."

I heard the door slam and waited a few minutes to make sure that they had gone before I came out of the larder, but when I emerged into the kitchen Richard was still there, leaning on the worktop, his head in his hands, shaken with painful sobbing. I hoped I could get past without his hearing me, but as I advanced into the room he looked up and saw me. I don't think I have ever seen such despair on a human face.

"I'm sorry," I said awkwardly, "I was in the larder. I couldn't help overhearing . . ."

I made as if to go away but he began to speak, softy at first but with increasing vehemence.

"I know what people think. I know you all think I'm a fool, and I suppose I am. But I can't help it. I love her so much . . ."

His voice broke and the tears came again. I moved over and put my hand on his arm.

"Don't, Richard," I said softly. "Don't distress yourself like this."

He made a great effort to pull himself together and took out a handkerchief to wipe his face.

"I'm so sorry, Sheila. This must be very embarrassing for you. I'm sorry."

"No," I protested. "No, please don't think that. It's just that I hate to see you so upset."

"I've loved her for so long, you see," he said quietly. "And there was a time, during the war, when I was in the RAF, when I thought she really cared for me. I suppose she thought it was quite glamorous, the uniform and everything. But then she met Bill and he was rich and important and I knew I didn't stand a chance. But after he died she seemed to need me." He looked at me pleadingly, but then he gave me a wry smile. "Of course, I was useful to her, that was all. . . . But the love was still there—*is* still there. Getting old," he said fiercely, "doesn't make the pain of rejection any less, that awful aching, wanting. You don't *feel* things less, you feel them more, because you know how little time there is left."

"Yes," I said, "I can see that."

He was quiet for a while and then he cried out, "She is so cruel! How can she be so unkind, so deliberately unkind? It's as if she enjoys seeing me suffer. How can she do that?"

"Some people are like that."

"This man, Laurence Marvell—she knows how worried I am about him, the sort of man he is, and she positively *flaunts* him. What do you think of him, Sheila?"

"I don't know, really. He seems very charming, very anxious to please."

"Anxious to worm his way into her confidence. Oh God! Why can't she see? She's infatuated with him, she won't listen . . ."

"I'm afraid people don't listen when they're infatuated."

"I know, I know." His voice was weary.

I looked at him and felt very sad. When I was young, Richard Lewis was one of the most sought-after men in Taviscombe. He was a different generation from me, the generation that had fought in the war. Richard had been a fighter pilot and, although he was too modest to talk about his wartime exploits, the fact that he'd been given the DFC spoke eloquently of his courage and made him a glamorous figure to my contemporaries. He'd been goodlooking, too, in a quiet sort of way, slim with fair hair and very blue eyes. Several of my friends had fancied themselves in love with him. But he was head over heels in love with Freda and had eyes for no one else. As he said, she had taken up with him for a while after the war, when he came back to Taviscombe as a war hero. But then Freda met Bill Spencer again (they'd met originally somewhere overseas during the war) and married him. His father was a merchant banker, extremely rich, so Bill was a tremendous catch. Poor Richard simply didn't stand a chance. Still didn't stand a chance.

I glanced at the elderly man standing beside me, stooping now, with thin grey hair, the blue eyes hidden behind spectacles and, today, looking for the first time quite frail, and I felt a wave of pity and sorrow that such a fine, intelligent man should have been reduced to this. I felt angry and longed to give Freda a piece of my mind, tell her how despicable her treatment of him had been. Though I knew that even if I plucked up the courage to do so, she would take no notice of what I or indeed anyone else had to say.

"I wish there was something I could do," I said. "Something I could say that might help."

"Sometimes I get angry," he said. "Sometimes I almost hate her. But then . . ."

"You should be angry," I said. "Don't let her ruin your life."

He laughed, a sad, bitter laugh. "It's too late for that now."

"No," I said vehemently. "It's never too late to start again."

"My dear Sheila, you're still young enough to believe that. My life is more or less over."

"That's nonsense! You're fit and well. There are all sorts of things you could do, places you could go."

"I have travelled, I have tried that. But wherever I go I always take Freda with me. The pain is still there. And it will be, I suppose, until I die. Or she does. Then, perhaps, I might be whole again. Do you know, when she was attacked and in the hospital and we didn't know how serious it was, I had this terrible thought."

He paused and looked at me. His eyes, although now behind spectacles, were still the same vivid blue. "I thought, If she dies, then I shall be free; I hope she dies."

He straightened up and moved towards the door. "I suppose we'd better lock up. I expect everyone else has gone."

I followed him out into the passage, still not quite believing what I had just heard.

Chapter Five

"I asked Olive Clark to lunch on Sunday," I said to Michael that evening. "Is that all right with you?"

"Fine." Michael cut himself a thick, rather crumbly piece of bread. "She's a nice old thing. We used to have good times when she took me out. It's funny, she seemed to enjoy those outings as much as I did. Really enjoyed, not just pretending to, like most grown-ups, but actually having fun, on my level, if you see what I mean."

"It's a sort of innocence of spirit," I replied. "If that doesn't sound too pompous. It's a rare quality. Anyway, she's looking forward to seeing you—she was very complimentary about your reading this afternoon."

"It did go well, didn't it?" Michael said. "Though, of course, Freda was the star of the show, with her bandaged head and all."

"Oh, *Freda*!" I said with some asperity.

"What do you mean, 'Oh, Freda!'?" Michael asked.

I gave him a brief resumé of the scene between Freda and Richard and what Richard had said to me afterwards.

"Good heavens! Poor old Richard. But for goodness sake, how could he be so upset? He's *ancient*. They both are!"

"Being old doesn't stop your having feelings," I said.

"But not feelings like that?" Michael said.

"It doesn't always work like that," I said, "as you will doubtless discover when *you* are old. No, Richard has never wavered in his feelings for Freda, we've all known that. But I never realised quite how vile she's been to him."

"Yes, well, she's a twenty-four-carat bitch."

"I just wish," I said viciously, cutting off a piece of cheese with unnecessary violence, "that someone would break her heart as she's broken Richard's."

I think Olive enjoyed her lunch with us. She and Michael reminisced happily about the old days. I'm always proud of the way Michael gets on so well with my elderly friends. He has a way of talking to them naturally without the sort of barriers that the young sometimes feel it necessary to erect when speaking to the old. I suppose this gentleness and understanding explain why he's being such a success in the Wills and Trusts department of his firm. I often wish Peter could see how well his son has turned out.

"That was when we went to the Bridgwater Carnival," Michael was saying. "Do you remember that enormous papier-mâché camel that came and loomed over us? I was really scared, but I didn't like to admit it, but then you said *you* were frightened of it so we went and had an ice cream. Several ice creams, I seem to remember!"

"It was a lovely day. I did enjoy it!" Olive smiled. "I wish I could take Emily's children to the carnival, but they live too far away."

"Yes, how are they all?" I asked. "Have you seen them lately?"

"Not for a while, but I'm going to spend Christmas with them. I'm really looking forward to that."

"I thought you usually spent Christmas with Freda," I said.

Her lips tightened into an unaccustomed hard line. "Not this year," she said. "Freda and Laurence are going to London for Christmas. Staying in a hotel."

"Ah," I said, "I see. Still," I went on brightly, "I

expect you'll have a nicer time with Emily, Ben, and the children."

"Oh yes," she agreed, her eyes lighting up. "Christmas is a time for the children, isn't it? I shall take some things with me, of course," she said confidentially. "An extra mouth to feed is quite an expense for them, poor dears. I was a bit worried about leaving Tinker." Tinker is Olive's cat, a fine, magisterial tabby, who is the light of her life. "But Betty—you know, Betty Slade who lives next door—will come in twice a day and feed him and make a fuss of him, and it's only for a few days."

"I don't think I'd like Christmas in a hotel," I said, "nor abroad like Sybil and Pauline. It wouldn't seem right somehow."

"You just like to make a martyr of yourself, slaving over the bread sauce and forcemeat stuffing," Michael said.

"Yes, well," I said defensively, "perhaps I do. But I still think Christmas is a time for families and being at home. Tradition and nostalgia all mixed up, memories of Christmas past and all that."

"After my mother died," Olive said, "Papa and I used to spend Christmas with Freda and her parents."

"What were they like?" I asked curiously.

"Oh, very sweet," Olive replied, "Aunt Bessie especially. So kind. Of course they adored Freda. In their eyes she could do no wrong. I suppose that's why she grew up so, well, *sure* of herself. She'd always been the centre of attention, you see, and greatly indulged. I used to envy her sometimes. Papa was a wonderful man, of course, but he was inclined to be rather stern. Of course if my mother had lived . . ."

"It sounds to me as if Freda was thoroughly spoiled," I said, "which is probably why she's so selfish."

"She has a very strong personality," Olive said mildly, "and she has this strong conviction that she is always right. Of course," she added with a little laugh, "she quite often is."

"I know," I said, "that's what makes it so maddening!" I got up from the table. "I hope you don't mind eating Christmas pudding *before* Christmas, but I made three this year and I thought I'd like to try one out before Hilda comes, to make sure it's all right. She's staying with us over the holiday, and she's very critical about food."

The puddings were all right and so was Christmas. Hilda was in an unexpectedly amiable mood, mainly because she had taken up knitting.

She spent every available moment executing complicated patterns, which involved numerous balls of different-coloured wool, which went rolling in all directions and had to be rescued from the excited attentions of Foss and the dogs. Apart from the irritation of the perpetual clicking of knitting needles (even during the Queen's speech), I was immensely grateful for this new preoccupation.

Hilda was greatly intrigued about the Freda/ Laurence situation. She had met Freda several times when she had been staying with us and had taken an instant dislike to her.

"Do you think there's anything *in* it?" she asked me when we were having coffee on Boxing Day morning. Michael had gone off on a Boxing Day shoot so we were alone.

"What do you mean? In it?"

"Oh, you know," she said impatiently, "anything like *that*?"

Hilda belongs to that generation that would not dream of calling a spade a spade.

"Oh, I see. Well, since Freda is old enough to be his mother and he's gay anyway, I wouldn't think so."

Hilda appeared dashed for a moment and then she said, "But they're staying in a hotel, aren't they? Not with friends or anything like that."

"So?"

"Well, then!"

"Oh Hilda, really! Staying in a hotel together doesn't mean anything!"

"No," she said grudgingly, "I suppose not. Still, you must admit that it's a very peculiar relationship."

"Not really. It's probably quite common, for all we know. A lonely old woman and a younger man who's prepared to pay her attention in exchange for the occasional gift or holiday. Why shouldn't she spend her money on Laurence, if that's what gives her pleasure?"

Hilda gave me a stern look. "But she shouldn't be lonely, should she? She has a daughter and grandchildren. Why should she turn to a stranger outside the family?"

Hilda was a great believer in the family.

"Well, they live quite a way away," I said. "Laurence is here in Taviscombe."

I felt irritated that I'd somehow been put in the position of defending a situation I didn't particularly approve of, but this is something that frequently happens when I have any sort of discussion with Hilda.

"And what does that cousin of hers think about it?"

"Olive? I don't think she approves. Of course

she's very loyal to Freda and wouldn't dream of actually saying anything, but I think she's unhappy about it. She and Freda used to spend a lot of time together, but now Laurence is around I don't think she sees nearly as much of her. And then, like you, she does feel that Freda ought to be reconciled with Emily—especially now there are the children."

"What sort of man is he?" Hilda asked. "I must say, I'd like to see him."

The opportunity for her to do so occurred a few days later. Laurence rang me in the morning with an invitation to tea. This was something that hadn't happened before and I was rather taken aback.

"That's very kind of you . . ." I began.

"I do apologise for such short notice," Laurence said, "but I'm afraid Freda is finding Taviscombe terribly *dull* after London, especially at this time of the year. I always think that the days between Christmas and New Year are absolutely *deadly*, don't you? So I thought I'd cheer her up with a little tea party. Do say you'll come!"

"It's very kind of you," I repeated, "but I have my cousin staying with me . . ."

"Marvellous! Bring her with you. A new face is just what Freda needs."

"Well," I said, "we'd love to."

"Lovely! Four o'clock, then. Do you know how to get to my cottage? Splendid. See you both later, then."

I noticed that Hilda dressed with unusual care for the tea party, even wearing the handsome cameo brooch that had belonged to her mother and which was only ever brought out on special occasions. I noted the phenomenon but didn't comment upon it.

Laurence Marvell lives in a small cottage on West Hill. Not one of the pricier thatched ones at the top of the hill, with a view of the bay below, but a tiny, slate-roofed artisan's cottage on the lower slopes, crammed in rather incongruously between two new ranch-style bungalows. Laurence greeted us enthusiastically.

"Do come in! It was so good of you to come at such short notice—though I always think the nicest things happen on the spur of the moment, don't you? Let me take your coats. It's really bitterly cold today. There now, here's the sitting room. Do go in."

Inside the cottage Laurence had certainly worked wonders. All the walls were white and the old doors had been painted black. The furniture was mostly Victorian and, as far as I could judge, very good, with many small ornaments and a few pleasant pictures. I was surprised, though, to recognise a very nice Pembroke table and an oak corner cupboard that I had last seen in Freda's house. There was a cheerful fire burning in the small, barred, Victorian grate and a table set for tea.

Freda, who was sitting in a chair by the fire, didn't get up (I felt Hilda bristle at this) but waved a languid hand in greeting. To my surprise the other person in the room was Richard.

"Do come and cheer us up," Freda said, "we've been so bored after all the excitements of London."

"You know my cousin Hilda," I said. "Richard, I don't know if you both met when she stayed with me before?"

Richard, who had risen, said at once, "Yes, indeed I do. Sheila brought you to the garden party at Brunswick Lodge last summer."

Hilda smiled approval at this courtesy and extended her hand graciously. "How nice of you to remember," she said.

Freda, bored with this exchange, said brusquely, "You're looking better than the last time I saw you, Hilda. Put on a bit of weight."

Hilda gave her a tight little smile. "Sheila tells me you had a nasty experience just before Christmas. You must take care of yourself, Freda, you look far from well."

I was beginning to wonder if it had been a good idea to bring Freda and Hilda together when Laurence came back into the room exuding goodwill.

"I thought we'd have nursery tea," he said, "so I've laid the table. I think the kettle's boiling so do sit down, everyone. Freda, you sit here and Sheila here and Hilda—so nice to meet you—*here,* next to Richard. That's fine. Freddie, will you be mother or shall I?"

Freda said, "Oh, you do it, Larry. Now do have one of these delicious scones, Sheila. Larry made them."

Larry, it appeared, had also made the two cakes—chocolate and lemon—as well as the shortbread biscuits. Larry was, obviously, a man of many talents.

Conversation, which might, in the circumstances, have been a bit strained, was carried along at first by Laurence and me, talking about the shows that he and Freda had seen in London, but gradually Hilda who, I was amused to see, was quite taken with Laurence, joined in and then Freda, unable to remain silent for long, held forth. Even Richard, who had, not unnaturally, regarded me with some embarrassment at first, volunteered several remarks, which Freda, apparently deciding to be amiable, refrained from contradicting as she usually did. To anyone looking in through the window we must have seemed the epitome of a happy, friendly, old-fashioned tea party.

"I did telephone Olive," Laurence said, "to see if she would like to come today, but there was no reply. I hope she's all right. There's been so much flu about just now."

"I expect she's still down with Emily," Hilda said. "She was spending Christmas there."

At the mention of Emily's name, the temperature dropped several degrees as Freda gave Hilda a furious look, which Hilda met with a bland stare, though I was sure that she knew perfectly well the effect her remark would have.

I broke in hastily, "Are you doing anything special for New Year's Eve, Laurence?"

"There's a dinner dance at the Grand in Exeter," he replied gratefully. "Freddie and I thought it might be rather fun."

"Do people still do proper dancing nowadays?" I asked. "Waltzes and foxtrots and things?"

"They do at the Grand," Laurence said. "We thought it would be nice to have an excuse to dress up—Freddie bought a divine new frock at Harrods, moiré taffeta, a sort of rich deep red, very nineteen-forties."

"Come to think of it, I did have a wine-coloured taffeta ball dress in the nineteen-forties,"

Freda said. "Do you remember, Richard? Just after the war. You gave me some of your clothing coupons for it just after you were demobbed." She laughed her distinctive, husky laugh. "God! The young today don't know they're born, do they? There we were *dying* for pretty clothes after all those years in uniform, but the clothes ration was so meagre, even if you could get black market coupons. And just look at young girls now—those dreary jeans and T-shirts, they make even the prettiest girls look plain!"

"But the uniforms," Laurence said, "in those old wartime movies, they were very attractive."

"Oh, the Wrens had the smartest uniforms," Freda said, "especially the Wren officers—those divine little tiddly hats! That's why all the girls were so keen to join." She looked around smugly. "It was the most difficult service to get into."

"Oh, I rather liked the Waaf uniform," I said.

"Oh no," Freda said pityingly. "Those awful air force blue stockings made everyone's legs look so fat! *Ours* were black. Very sexy!"

Hilda turned a disapproving gaze upon her. "I have no doubt they did a more valuable job than girls who were only concerned with their appearance."

"And what did *you* do in the war, Hilda?"

Freda asked with deceptive sweetness. "You weren't in the forces, were you?"

"Actually," Hilda said, "I was at Bletchley, doing decoding work."

There was a moment's silence while we mentally chalked up a point for Hilda.

"That must have been very interesting," Laurence said. "Do tell us about it."

Hilda gave him a little smile. "Oh, I can't do that," she said smugly. "We had to sign the Official Secrets Act, you know, and in any case it isn't the subject for idle chatter."

"No, of course," Laurence said meekly. "And what are you and Sheila doing for the New Year?"

"I have to go back to London tomorrow," Hilda said. "I never like to leave the house too long at this time of the year. I shall, of course, be going to the watch-night service at St. Margaret's, as I always do."

"And you, Sheila," Laurence said, "are you going to St. James's?"

"I'm afraid not," I said. "I find it really difficult to keep awake that long. When Peter was alive we sometimes used to go. Michael is going to the Bancrofts' party but I cried off. Nowadays the thought of going to a party which you know you can't possibly leave until after midnight absolutely appalls me!"

On New Year's Eve I went to bed at my usual time and fell asleep over my book as I so often do. I awoke with a start to hear the grandfather clock in the hall striking the hour and then the sound of bells, carried across the still night air from St. James's, ringing in the new year.

Like most people of my age I found my thoughts turning back to the past, rather than forward to the year to come. Another year had gone; where had it gone to? Another year without Peter, but another year with Michael, watching him grow in maturity. A good year, on the whole.

> The year is dying in the night;
> Ring out, wild bells, and let him die.

Did people ever read Tennyson nowadays, I wondered? My book fell to the floor and, as I moved to pick it up, Foss, lying on my feet at the end of the bed, raised his head, gave me a reproachful look, and composed himself once more to sleep.

Chapter Six

"Come on," Rosemary said. "New year, new beginning. I've got the application forms for the swimming club at the Westwood."

"Oh, all right," I agreed reluctantly. "But nothing is going to get me into that gym."

Indeed, the gymnasium at the Westwood was very formidable with rowing machines, treadmills, and exercise bicycles of every kind of complexity. Looking at all the paraphernalia apparently necessary to keep the human form in shape, I decided I preferred to remain the (rather inelegant) shape that I was. The pool was next to the gym, and they were both housed in a kind of annexe, which you entered through the main hotel. It was a pleasant place with large windows, looking out onto the gardens and the sea beyond, with a steam room in an alcove on one side and a jacuzzi, raised up on a sort of throne, on the other. The changing rooms were at either end and I was pleased to find that the whole place was agreeably warm in contrast to the cold January day outside.

After a few visits we learnt to avoid the times when Freda and Laurence were there. They both went in for a very splashy kind of crawl, which looked highly professional but, given the relatively small size of the pool, was not very popular with the other bathers. After a little experimenting we found the pleasantest time to go was in the late morning when there were only a few people, mostly elderly ladies, progressing with a stately breast-stroke slowly up and down the pool. Sometimes, indeed, when Rosemary was busy and everybody else had gone to lunch, I had the whole place to myself. Then I was able to trundle up and down with my old-fashioned side-stroke, mindlessly enjoying the sheer pleasure of moving through the water.

One afternoon, after a tiresome morning trying in vain to write an intelligent review of a particularly obscure book about the Female Image in the novels of Henry James, I felt the need for a little relaxation. I arrived at the Westwood just as an ambulance was pulling away. There was no one on the reception desk, but by the door leading to the pool I saw one of the hotel staff that I knew.

"Hello, Denise," I greeted her. "I saw an ambulance as I was coming in. Has there been an accident?"

She looked harassed. "Oh, Mrs. Malory, were you going to the pool? I'm afraid there's a bit of a problem." She picked up the wooden board on a stand that said POOL OPEN and turned it round so that it now read POOL CLOSED.

"I'm ever so sorry," she said, indicating the notice, "but, like I said, there's been some trouble."

"What happened?"

"One of the ladies had a nasty turn in the steam room. She collapsed, but fortunately someone found her . . ."

"Good heavens!" I said. "How awful. Is she all right?"

"Oh yes, but Mr. Hardy, the manager, thought we'd better get an ambulance just in case. Well, she is quite elderly. I think you know her—a Mrs. Spencer."

"Freda? That's terrible! You're sure she's all right?"

"Well, she'd come round before the ambulance arrived. She said we were making a fuss about nothing, but you could see she was quite shaken."

"They've taken her to the cottage hospital, I suppose?"

"That's right."

"I think perhaps I'll just go along there now and see if there's anything I can do."

Freda was already in a bed on one of the wards when I got to the hospital. She was wearing a hospital gown and looking extremely annoyed.

"Ah, Sheila," she said irritably. "Will you please drive me home at once. There is absolutely no need for me to stay in this horrible place overnight. That stupid Dr. Macdonald is making a ridiculous fuss about nothing. Surely I am the best judge of how I feel!"

"Dr. Macdonald is only trying to make sure you're all right," I said soothingly. "There might be side effects or anything . . ."

"Rubbish!"

"How did it happen?"

"I just got too hot in that steam room—I'd been in the gym for a session beforehand—that door's very heavy and the wretched handle stuck so I couldn't get it open and I was feeling a bit groggy anyway so I suppose I must have passed out for a moment. So you see there's absolutely no need for all this absurd nonsense."

"I'm sure they know what they're doing," I said. "They don't want to take any risks. Now would you like me to fetch you anything from home, a nightdress and toothbrush?"

Freda ignored my question. "Why isn't Laurence here?" she demanded pettishly. "I told them to ring him as soon as they brought me here."

"Perhaps he's out," I suggested.

Freda gave me a look of withering dislike. "He'd better get my things, I suppose, if I *have* to stay here. He's got a key and he knows where everything is . . ." She broke off as Laurence came hurrying down the ward.

"Freddie, darling, what's happened? I've only just got your message."

"Where have you been?" she demanded.

"Don't you remember, darling," he said, drawing a chair up to her bedside, "I went into Taunton to get that embroidery silk you wanted. I've only just got back and there was this message on the answerphone."

"Oh yes, the silk." She seemed slightly mollified. "Did you get the deep pink and that special green?"

"I got the pink, but they're going to have to order the green."

An expression of displeasure crossed her face. "How tiresome! I wanted to get on with that."

"Oh, never mind the embroidery!" Laurence exclaimed impatiently. "Tell me what happened. Are you all right?"

Instead of insisting that it was all a fuss about nothing, Freda suddenly assumed an expression of suffering bravely borne. "Oh, it's nothing, *really,*" she said, her voice quavering slightly.

"But they said you'd collapsed!"

"Well, I'd had *quite* a session on that road-walking thing in the gym and then a work-out with those weights. So I thought a nice sit-down in the steam room before I had a swim."

"For goodness sake!" Laurence exclaimed, "You shouldn't push yourself like that."

"Nonsense, I'm perfectly fit. Anyway, I sat there and turned up the heat a bit. But then I seemed to get very hot and rather dizzy and I tried to open the door and the wretched thing stuck, and while I was wrestling with it I suppose I passed out. The next thing I knew I was out of the steam room and lying by the pool and Patrick—you know, the young man who looks after the pool—and the hotel manager were wrapping me in towels and forcing glasses of water on me."

"Good God! How lucky they found you. It could have been very serious."

"They insisted on calling an ambulance," Freda went on, "although I told them I was perfectly all right. Oh yes. You'll have to go and collect my car, Larry. It's still in the car park there."

"And what about the door? Of the steam room, I mean. You say it was stuck. That's really very bad. What did they have to say about that?"

"They *said* it was perfectly all right and that I'd been pulling the handle the wrong way."

"Well," he said, "I daresay you might have been a bit confused under the circumstances—the heat and being exhausted and everything. Still . . ."

"Well, never mind that now," Freda interrupted him. "Since everyone seems determined I have to stay in this ghastly place overnight, you'd better go and get some things for me."

I got up. "I'll be off then, Freda, if there's nothing I can do. I do hope you'll be quite all right tomorrow."

"I'm quite all right *now,*" she snapped. "Now, Larry, get a piece of paper and I'll give you a list."

Laurence rose from his chair. "Thank you for coming, Sheila. It was very good of you."

"Yes," Freda echoed perfunctorily, "very good. Now, Larry, that paper . . ."

I walked out of the ward and, just outside, I ran into Cynthia Fellows, one of the Hospital Friends who wanted to tell me about the new library service and ask if I had any books to spare, and by the time I'd escaped from her, Laurence had been dismissed by Freda and had caught me up.

"Oh, Sheila," he said, "I hoped I might get a word with you. It was so good of you to come. How did you hear about it?"

"I went to swim at the Westwood," I said, "and they'd just taken Freda away in an ambulance. So I came over here right away to see how she was."

"It could have been very nasty," he said. "She should never have done that work-out. It's quite ridiculous. Sometimes when we're there together she does more than I do."

"Freda's always been very competitive," I said, "and she hates to think of herself as elderly in any way. I mean, she really is remarkable for her age."

"Yes, she is a bit sensitive about that." He laughed. "It's funny, really. She keeps going on about the Wrens and the war but she won't admit how old she is!"

"Oh well, perhaps we all need a bit of harmless vanity to keep us going."

"As long as she doesn't overdo it. But to do all that and then go into the steam room! She knows it always makes her dizzy. And then that business with the door; I suppose she had a bit of a panic attack. It could have been very nasty. Do you know how long she'd been unconscious?"

"No, I'm sorry, I don't. The young man who looks after the pool found her slumped on the floor of the steam room. She could have been there quite a while."

Laurence gave a weary sigh. "What will she get up to next? Oh well, I'd better get a move on and fetch those things for her. Thank you again, Sheila."

He waved his hand in farewell and ran quickly down the stairs. I was struck by his proprietorial air—a son looking after his mother, a husband looking after his wife. But Laurence was neither of these things. He had a key, I had noted, and would know where everything was in Freda's house. Well, it was nothing to do with me. I went, more slowly, down the stairs, left the hospital, and wandered aimlessly round the fiction shelves of the public library looking for something that would provide a little light relief from the perplexing business of living.

Rosemary rang me that evening. "Maureen Philips says, have you got any school photos?" she asked. "Because she's mounting an exhibition for the reunion. I've got the one of our last year, but I can't find any of the others. I have a feeling Mother threw them away because I looked so untidy in them. She was always on at me about it."

"Yes, I'm sure I've still got a couple, but I've got

a horrid feeling they're up in the loft somewhere. I'll have to get Michael to ferret around. I really can't manage that ladder any more. In the unlikely event of my ever moving from this house, the contents of the loft will have to remain as part of the fixtures and fittings."

"Oh, I know. It's extraordinary what you collect up there. We managed to find Jilly's old playpen when Delia was born. Jack did it up and it's been a godsend. Anyway, do see what you can find. Maureen needs them right away because the reunion's next week. She wondered if Freda or Olive have any photos of their year, just before the war. If you see Freda, could you ask her?"

"Well, she's in hospital at the moment, but she should be out tomorrow if everything's all right."

"In hospital?"

I explained what had happened.

"What a ghastly thing! But typical of Freda—ridiculous to go on like that at her age. It's lucky she hasn't got a dicky heart, otherwise she'd have died!"

"Oh, Freda's immortal," I laughed. "Actually I might be seeing Olive at the Antiquarians' meeting tomorrow, so I'll ask her then about the photos."

After supper I sent Michael up into the loft to look for the photos. He came down with a great boxfull and I spent a sentimental evening going through them. Photographs of Peter in his army uniform, doing his national service, Michael as a baby, Michael as a small boy (hundreds of those), pictures of holidays at home and abroad, pictures of every animal we have ever owned, even a photograph of me in a Mary Quant miniskirt and high white boots, which caused Michael much mirth. Right at the bottom of the box I found a couple of school groups, sepia with age. I unrolled them carefully and studied them with amusement. There was Rosemary at the end of the second row down—her dark hair escaping wispily from the ribbon that tied it back and blowing across her face. I was standing next to her, a stolid child with short hair and a fringe. For some reason we both seemed to be shaking with suppressed laughter and I suddenly remembered that we had been standing on benches from the gym and the boys standing at the other end were trying to rock them up and down, which seemed to us all to be exquisitely funny. I smiled affectionately at my younger self and put the photos to one side.

When I was young a school reunion had seemed the ultimate in boredom, but, growing older, I had come to value this chance to look back at the past, at the person I once was, to see how we had all turned out. I thought of Freda and Olive. I hadn't had much to do with them when I was young, they had seemed like another generation—well, I suppose they were—but as time goes by the generations merge and now they seemed almost like my contemporaries. Freda had always stood out. Her undeniable good looks, together with her forceful personality, made her the focus of any gathering. I didn't remember her during the war, of course, but my mother used to tell me with some amusement how she used to peacock around Taviscombe in her Wrens' uniform on her early leaves. Later in the war she was abroad and then she married Bill Spencer and hardly ever came home to visit her parents. She was in America when her father died but she did come back for her mother's funeral, re-organising everything and changing all the arrangements that poor Olive had tried to make to try to spare Freda the distress she obviously didn't feel.

I had really only known her in fairly recent years when she returned to give Taviscombe the full force of her energy and her brisk organisational ability. People complained about how she rode rough-shod over other people, but although I found Freda herself disagreeable, I had had enough to do with voluntary organisations to know that, whether we like it or not, it is the Fredas of this world who keep things going, and that without them everything would fall apart.

Chapter Seven

"Have you *seen* Pamela Nelson?" Sybil exclaimed. "No, of course, she would have left by the time you were at school."

"I vaguely remember her," I said. "Her father used to have that newsagents in the Avenue, didn't he, where Boots is now?"

"So he did. I'd quite forgotten. I haven't seen Pam for years. She nursed with Pauline at St. Mary's Paddington in the blitz and she stayed on there after the war, married one of the doctors."

"So what's she like now?" I asked.

"A lot of *very* blonde hair done up on top of her head and a great deal of make-up. A dressy, silk two-piece thing and ridiculous high heels. So silly at our age!"

"Oh well," I said tolerantly, "I suppose everyone feels they have to make a bit of an effort for a school reunion."

"I don't," Sybil said firmly.

I looked at her blue button-through summer dress that appeared, like all Sybil's clothes, more like a uniform than an item of civilian clothing, at her too-heavy sensible shoes, at her face innocent of make-up, and her grey, wiry hair cut in a short, uncompromising bob. "No nonsense" was how Sybil was accustomed to describe her attitude to her appearance, and no nonsense it certainly was.

"Yes, well," I said diplomatically, "there are more important things than clothes. So how is she, Pam Nelson?"

"I don't know, I haven't spoken to her yet. I was so taken aback by what she looked like! There she is, talking to Pauline. I'll just go and have a word."

I looked at the tall woman talking to Sybil's sister. Certainly she was very striking and, from a distance, extremely well preserved. I heard a muffled exclamation just behind me and turned to find Freda staring at the little group.

"For God's sake! Just look at Pam Nelson," she said. "Making a spectacle of herself as usual!"

"She does look splendid, doesn't she?" I asked provocatively. "She appears to have gone blonde since I knew her. I seem to remember her with light brown hair."

"It looks like a wig to me," Freda said.

"I wonder if that's her husband? Do you see, that tall, rather distinguished grey-haired man talking to Pauline now?"

"I haven't the faintest idea," Freda said dismissively. "I must go and have a word with Elizabeth Sewell. She was *very* high up in the Civil Service, you know."

I remembered that my mother told me that Freda and Pam had been rivals of some sort, vying with each other before the war, as to who had the latest fashion, who had the most sought-after boyfriend. It would seem that old passions, with Freda at least, died hard. I wondered if Pamela felt the same way.

It seemed strange, wrong almost, to be standing in what used to be the geography room with a glass of white wine in my hand. I said as much to Rosemary.

"Oh, I know. I keep expecting Miss Jacques to come up behind me and say, 'And what do you think *you're* doing, Rosemary Dudley,' like she used to."

"And everywhere looks smaller, of course, and the new bits are horrid—that language laboratory and the computer room. I know it's progress, but I can't help feeling resentful that they've changed things, canceled out our memories."

Rosemary reached over and took two new glasses of wine from a tray on one of the desks. "Here," she said, "drink this and cheer up."

"Another thing that's odd," I said, "is the way people aren't like you remember."

Rosemary looked at me enquiringly.

"You know how we used to *hate* Dorothy Welsh? Well, I ran into her just now and she was awfully nice, very cosy and quite witty. I couldn't believe it."

"Perhaps she's changed," Rosemary suggested.

"Mm, perhaps, but perhaps she was always like that underneath and we never bothered to find out. Just took her at face value. I wonder how often we do that in life?"

"For goodness sake, don't go all philosophical on me! I've already had Mavis Benson practically in tears in the gym remembering the crush she used to have on Miss Field. Come on, let's go and look at the photos. They're always good for a laugh."

Certainly the long gym slips and stiff, awkward hairstyles of the prewar group photographs did make us smile.

"There now," I said. "Look, there's Pam Nelson, there, at the front with the prefects. She *did* have brown hair. But she was pretty! Even in that ridiculous shirt and tie and her hair in a plait.

Prettier than Freda; there *she* is, next to Dr. Gibbs. She was head girl—naturally, she would be."

"Look," Rosemary said, leaning forward to examine the group more closely. "There's Richard. Looking very glamorous. Oh, it's such a wicked waste that Freda got her clutches into him like that! And there's Toby Longworth—he was a sort of second cousin of mine. He was killed at Arnhem."

"A lot of the boys on that photo never came back." Richard was standing behind us. "Dick Parsons, Maurice Green, Clive Webber . . ." He broke off and turned away. We watched him go out of the room.

"Oh Lord!" Rosemary said. "Do you think he heard? What I said about him and Freda?"

"Well," I replied, "if he did he wouldn't be surprised. He must know what everyone thinks by now."

"Still, I do hope he *didn't* hear. He's so nice and I'd hate to have hurt his feelings. Oh well. Perhaps we ought to go down into School Hall, it's almost time for the speeches. Let's cut through the cloisters."

The cloisters are not as grand as their name suggests, being merely a covered way, open on one side, linking the classrooms with School Hall. When I pushed open the swing doors leading to the cloisters, we saw Freda and Pam Nelson standing at the other end. They seemed to be having a heated argument, but when they saw us they broke off and watched us pass by in silence.

As we went through the doors into School Hall Rosemary turned to me and said, "What on earth do you think that was all about?"

"It looked as if they were having a bit of a disagreement."

"A flaming row, more like! Pam was obviously livid about something. I wonder what it was."

"I believe there was always bad feelings between them."

"But surely, after all this time! Oh well, I don't suppose we'll ever know. How frustrating! Oh look, there's Olive. Let's go and sit by her. I hope the speeches don't go on too long. I want to go home and get changed for tonight."

That evening at the reunion dinner I made a point of watching Freda and Pam, but they seemed to be avoiding each other and I saw no contact between them. I asked Pauline, who was sitting next to me, about Pam.

"She gave up nursing when she got married, of course. I believe they live in Surrey, a rather grand house, I think, but of course he was very eminent in his field—paediatrics—and he lectured a lot in America before he retired. Pam went with him quite often. There weren't any children—ironic, really. But she's had a very interesting life."

"Well," I said, "so have you. That time in India in the war and all the globetrotting you do with Sybil."

"Luke, my husband, didn't care to go abroad," Pauline confided. "He was delicate, you know, and couldn't stand hot climates. And travelling with Sybil is really very tiresome. She has absolutely no idea about comfort. If I *told* you about some of the dreadful places we've stayed in! No, Pam always travelled first class, in every sense of the word."

"She and Freda never got on, did they?" I asked.

Pauline laughed. "Oh, my dear! If you could have seen them when we were all young. Talk about catty. Well, really *bitchy*!" She brought out the stronger word self-consciously. Pauline always did have a tendency to put a ladylike gloss on things. Her use of such a word indicated the strength of feeling she wanted to convey.

"Really?"

"Oh yes. In their last year they were both in the running for head girl but Pam got into some sort of trouble—I don't remember what it was—and Freda got it. And then, later, at the beginning of the war, Pam was practically engaged to Richard, you know, when Freda took him off her."

"No! I never knew that!"

"Oh, whatever Pam had Freda wanted. Don't you remember, Sybil?" She leaned across the table to address her sister. "How Freda took Richard off Pam?"

"Good God, yes, so she did. I'd forgotten that. Well, I don't know if she took him off her exactly, but she certainly stepped in pretty quickly when Pam went up to London to St. Mary's. Poor Richard. Between them, he never stood a chance!"

I looked round anxiously. Sybil's voice was very penetrating, even in the general hubbub. Fortunately, Richard was at the far end of the room, having managed to get a seat next to Freda, but, since she was talking animatedly to the man on her other side (Henry Chadwick, a circuit judge and one of our most distinguished old boys, and how like Freda to nobble him!), he looked pretty miserable. I thought how sad it must be to have given all your affection to someone who not only gave you nothing in return but who seemed intent on making you an object of universal ridicule and pity.

I was surprised that Freda hadn't made Laurence come to the reunion, since other people had brought guests. I said as much to Sybil, who said, "I wouldn't think it was his sort of thing, would you? Anyway, I don't suppose Freda wants him to realise that she's as ancient as we are."

After the dinner, when people were mingling, I saw Pam Nelson approach Richard and they walked away together into a small conservatory that led out of the dining room. I moved over to where I could see them standing beside a large palm deep in conversation, and I longed to know what they were saying to each other. After a while Pam came back into the dining room. Richard stood there for a little longer, then slowly followed her.

As he came into the room Freda went up to him and I heard her say, "Richard, here are my keys. Go and get my scarf from the car for me. It's not really very warm in here."

He looked at her blankly and was silent so that Freda said sharply, "Richard! My scarf!"

He suddenly seemed to focus and said coldly, "I'm sorry, Freda, I'm going now," and turned and walked away.

I don't think I've ever seen anyone as taken aback as Freda. It was as if a dove had suddenly flown up and pecked her in the face. When she realised that I had overheard the exchange, she flushed scarlet with fury and mortification. Then she turned on her heel and marched over to the far side of the room where she interrupted the conversation of two people she hardly knew, who seemed surprised at her sudden intrusion. I suddenly realised how tired I was. The room was crowded and the effort of trying to hear conversations against a background of laughter and raised voices was making my head ache. I went over to where Rosemary was talking to Pauline.

"I'm off now," I said. "It's been lovely seeing everyone but I really don't think I can take in another word, I'm absolutely done in."

"I know," Rosemary replied sympathetically. "I can't think how some of the older ones can keep it up. Just look at Mrs. Fernley." She indicated our old French teacher, who was talking animatedly to a group of former pupils. "She must be well into her eighties, but she's fresh as a daisy!"

"It's a generation thing," I said. "Think of your mother."

Rosemary groaned. "Don't!" she said. "Anyway, there'll still be quite a few people around tomorrow—coffee at Brunswick Lodge at eleven in the morning, remember, and then the concert in the evening."

"Yes," I said. "Of course. I'll catch up with

some of the others then." I waved goodbye to Pauline and made my way out of the hotel.

The Esplanade Hotel, as its name implies, is on the sea-front. As I walked towards my car I glanced across to see if the tide was in. A man was leaning on the sea wall and in the light of the street lamp I saw that it was Richard. Something about his attitude alarmed me and I crossed the road and went up to him.

"Richard! Are you all right?"

His back was towards me but as I spoke he turned round. He looked terrible. This time there were no tears, but instead a sort of numb pain, even more distressing to see.

"Richard!" I repeated, now really alarmed. "What on earth's the matter?"

He looked at me unseeingly and then, slowly focusing, he seemed to recover himself a little. "Sheila," he said tentatively, as if not certain of my name. "Sheila . . . yes, thank you. I'm all right."

"Are you sure?"

"Yes, yes. Please. Forgive me, there's something I have to think about. I just want to be alone to sort things out."

"Yes, of course." I retreated a few steps. "If you're sure . . ."

"Yes. Thank you. Thank you for being concerned."

He turned away, looked out to sea again, at the lights across the Channel in Wales, looking, perhaps, back into the past, which is also another country.

Chapter Eight

Quite a few old pupils seemed to have stayed on for the second day. The coffee morning at Brunswick Lodge was very well attended and I managed to catch up with several people I hadn't spoken to the day before. I was just thinking of going when I saw Pam Nelson standing by herself looking out of the window. I went over to join her.

"Hello, Pam," I said. "I don't suppose you remember me. Sheila Malory—Sheila Prior that was."

She turned and smiled. "Yes, I think I do. You were much younger than me, but I do remember you. I remember your father very well. I used to go to his confirmation classes. I thought they'd be very boring, but he made them so interesting and really good fun. And your mother, too. She always gave us cake and lemonade afterwards."

"Goodness, yes, I'd quite forgotten that!" I exclaimed, memories coming back to me of laughter coming from behind the closed doors of my father's study and of helping my mother to set out the jug of home-made lemonade and the glasses on the tray. "How extraordinary of you to remember after all this time."

"Your father was very kind when my brother Jack was killed at Dunkirk. I remember that. I was so sorry to hear that your father had died and about your mother's illness, too. My parents kept me up to date with Taviscombe news, of course. Now let me see, you married that good-looking Malory boy, the one with the gorgeous fair, curly hair. How is he?"

"Peter? I'm afraid he died several years ago."

"I'm so sorry."

"My son, Michael, has fair, curly hair too," I said. "He's a solicitor in Peter's old practice."

"That's nice."

There was a slightly embarrassed silence and then I said, "Are you staying for the concert this evening?"

"Yes," she replied. "I thought we might as well make a weekend of it. I've got this very old uncle living in a nursing home on West Hill. I've got to visit him this afternoon. He's pretty well gaga, probably won't remember me after all these years, but while I'm here I thought I'd go."

"Does your husband know Taviscombe at all?"

"Jim? He came down with me for Mother's funeral, but we didn't have time to stay."

"Pauline was telling me yesterday that he's very eminent in his field."

"Was. He's been retired for a couple of years now . . ." She broke off as Richard came into the room. "Look, will you excuse me? I'd just like to have a word with someone. It's been lovely talking to you."

She went over and said something to Richard that I couldn't hear and they both went out of the room.

I picked up my handbag and was just preparing to leave when Freda buttonholed me. She had a list in her hand and seemed annoyed about something.

"Ah, Sheila. Perhaps you can tell me where Evelyn Parrish is? She was *supposed* to be helping Maureen with the washing up and she's completely disappeared."

"I'm sorry . . ."

"I made a perfectly clear roster for the people who said they were prepared to help. It is very disheartening when it is not adhered to!" She waved the list with an irritable gesture and went on in her best quarterdeck manner, "I've got a thousand and one things to do today and I won't have time if I can't get the clearing up here off my slop-chit."

"The reunion has been a great success, hasn't it?" I said, trying to change the subject.

Freda refused to be diverted. "Yes, I suppose so," she said impatiently. "Then, of course, there's all the preparation to do for the concert. You are bringing the canapés at four o'clock?"

"Well, about then . . ."

"Make sure that they are properly covered up if you leave them on the work-top in the kitchen. There are some tea-towels you can use for that in the top right-hand drawer. And Lionel is coming in early to make his special punch, so that it just has to be warmed through before the interval. Did Jean bring her punch bowl?" She consulted her list. "Oh yes, she did that this morning. I shall be here straight after lunch—there are several things I have to do myself. So I will be able to let you in. Or, if I'm delayed for any reason, Lionel will do so. As a committee member he has a key to the back door. Oh yes, and I want to make a notice for the door of the Museum Room."

"A notice?"

"Yes. We can't have people wandering in and

out of there in the interval without proper supervision and I will be far too busy to do that."

"But surely," I protested, "the people who are coming to the concert aren't likely to do anything awful to the exhibits, even if they *aren't* supervised."

"That may be your opinion, Sheila, but I know better. There are some valuable artefacts there. I shall put a notice on the door saying 'No Admittance.' " She made a note on her list.

"Is Laurence coming this evening?" I asked.

"No, he's been in London for a few days and won't be back until quite late."

"In London?"

"Yes, his aunt isn't well again. She sounds a very *demanding* woman, I must say, and poor Laurence is very good to her. He has such a sweet nature, so kind and considerate to everyone. He's been back and forth to see her quite a lot lately."

"I see."

I thought it highly probable that Laurence's sweet nature was inspired by the possibility of a legacy—if, indeed, there really *was* an aunt.

"Meanwhile," Freda said briskly, "there are still all the chairs here to be re-arranged for this evening and the trestle tables taken down. Where's Richard? He's supposed to be in charge of that. People are starting to leave and he should be on hand to see to things."

"Richard *was* here," I said. And then, deliberately, to see what her reaction would be, I added, "He went out a few minutes ago with Pam Nelson."

She stood absolutely still, something very like fear in her eyes. "With Pam Nelson?" she echoed.

"Yes."

For a moment it seemed as if she was going to say something, then, without another word, she turned and went out of the room.

I was still wondering what it was all about as I opened tins of anchovies and mashed up sardines after lunch. Something was going on, that was obvious. But what old feuds and passions would still have the power to rouse such emotions (and emotions had palpably been aroused) after more than fifty years? I said as much to Michael who was spraying wax on his Barbour jacket.

"Can't imagine," he said. "They're all as old as Methuselah anyway. What about 'all passion spent' and that kind of thing?"

"Perhaps in some cases it never is spent, however old you are. Oh, darling, do be careful with that spray. A light layer of wax is *not* going to improve these canapes!"

"Sorry—I've nearly finished. You say old Freda Thing was really put out?"

"Very much so." I prised the lid off a tub of taramasalata. "I've never seen her look like that before. And Richard's behaving oddly too. He was really rude to her last night."

"Good heavens!"

"It's obviously something to do with Pam Nelson. I do wish I could remember more about her."

"Ask Mrs. Dudley."

Mrs. Dudley, Rosemary's mother, is the fountainhead of all Taviscombe gossip, past and present.

"I might do that, if I can summon up the energy to go to tea with her—she asked me ages ago and I've been putting it off. One does need to feel very *strong* before embarking on that particular enterprise. Still," I went on, "even if Freda did take Richard away from Pam, it's all a long time ago and Pam seems to be perfectly happily married now, and to a very distinguished man, a top London consultant with an international reputation. Very different from poor Richard."

Richard, now retired, had made a modest living as an architect, based in Bristol.

"Oh well," Michael said, "if there's a skeleton in anyone's cupboard, Mrs. Dudley will know."

He took a small biscuit which I had just spread

with pâté and crammed it whole into his mouth. "Right then," he said indistinctly, "I'm off now. A clay shoot with Jonah."

"I've just got to deliver these to Brunswick Lodge," I said, "and then I'll come back and get changed for the concert. I don't expect I'll be home much before ten-thirty, so can you forage for yourself this evening?"

"That's all right, Ma, we're going on to Taunton afterwards so we'll probably get a curry or something." He gathered up his jacket and was gone.

I packed the canapés neatly on trays, covered them with cling-film, and, evading the inquisitive attention of the dogs, put them into the boot of the car and drove to Brunswick Lodge.

There were two cars in the car-park; one was Freda's, the other I assumed to be Lionel's. I went round to the back door and rang the bell. There was no reply. After a while I rang again.

I heard footsteps and then a man's voice called out in an agitated manner, "Who is it? Who's there?"

"It's me, Sheila Malory," I called back, feeling rather foolish, as you do when shouting your name out loud. "Is that you, Lionel?"

The door opened.

"Thank God! Something terrible's happened and I don't know what to do!" Lionel Prentiss is a small man, in his late sixties, and fright (he was obviously terrified of something) made him seem even smaller.

"Lionel! What's the matter? What's happened?"

For a moment he was silent, simply shaking his head in distress, as if whatever it was that had happened had deprived him of the power of speech.

"Lionel," I said again, "tell me. What's *happened*?"

"I can't," he burst out. "Here, see for yourself!"

He walked ahead of me along the narrow passage that leads to the Museum Room. He opened the door and stood back for me to enter.

Freda was lying on the floor. Her legs were twisted under her and there was blood seeping slowly onto the floor from a wound in her side. Her eyes were open and she was obviously quite dead.

Instinctively, I took a step towards her, stupidly stretching out my hand as if there was something I could do. I felt dreadfully cold and found that I was shaking. My mind refused to work, refused even to accept the visible proof of the terrible scene confronting me. A sort of blankness descended on me, blocking out the reality of what had happened so that I stood transfixed, like a statue, dumb witness to a dreadful act. I was brought back to myself by Lionel Prentiss, stronger, more articulate now that he had someone with whom to share the nightmare.

"Is she dead? What should we do?"

With a great effort I pulled myself together and turned to face him. He was standing in the doorway, unwilling to enter the room, his gaze fixed on me rather than on the still figure on the floor.

"Do?" I repeated dully.

I noted in a detached way that his face was a greyish putty colour, presumably from fright, almost the colour of his greyish hair.

"Do?" I made a great effort of will and concentrated. "We must phone the police. I'll use the phone in the office."

As I left the room he followed close on my heels, as the dogs do when they are frightened in a thunderstorm and need the reassurance of my company. I dialed 999 and told the duty sergeant what had happened. He said that someone would be along right away and we weren't to touch anything.

I repeated this to Lionel, who said with a shudder, "I didn't touch her, perhaps I should have but I couldn't . . ."

"There was nothing anyone could do for her," I said. "She must have been dead for a little while."

"I haven't been here long," he said. "I came to make the punch. I let myself in at the back door and I was going through to the kitchen when I passed the Museum Room and . . . saw her. The door was open, you see."

"Did you go into the room?" I asked.

He shook his head. "No, it was such a shock. I couldn't think what to do. I was frightened. I thought the person who—you know—I thought someone might still be here."

"You didn't hear anything?"

"No, it was silent as the . . ." He gulped. "No, I didn't hear anything."

"And the back door was locked?"

"Oh yes, I told you. I opened it with my key. I was going to ring the front door bell—I mean, I saw Freda's car in the car park. But then, I thought that if she was busy she might be annoyed at being disturbed. You know what she's like." He stopped, embarrassed at having spoken ill of the dead.

"Yes," I said, "I know." I moved to the door.

"Where are you going?" Lionel asked.

"The Museum Room," I said. "Someone should have a look at things before the police arrive, see if anything's missing, if it was a burglary."

"Yes, well, forgive me, I don't think I could. You'll think it's silly of me, Mrs. Malory, but I really can't. It's been such a shock . . ."

"Of course," I said. "You stay here."

He seemed to make an effort to resume some sort of normal behaviour. "Perhaps I should go into the kitchen," he suggested, "and make a start on the punch."

"I don't think we'll be needing the punch," I said gently. "I don't think there'll be a concert this evening—not after what's happened."

I went into the Museum Room. It was quite warm in there in contrast to the rest of Brunswick Lodge. I bent to feel the extra heater that Freda had insisted should be installed to protect the exhibits. It was hot. Freda must have switched it on when she arrived.

The room was quite large, with glass cases arranged round two sides, containing old coins, pottery, a flint axe, part of a Bronze Age brooch, a few mediaevel artefacts—the usual antique bric-a-brac, in fact, of any small-town museum. Round the two remaining walls were hung old agricultural implements, rusty reminders of Taviscombe's rural past. Nothing seemed to have been disturbed. I checked the windows. Nothing had been forced.

I came slowly back to the end of the room where Freda was lying beside the desk. Forcing myself to look more closely, I saw her handbag was on the floor by the desk, in full view of anyone who came into the room. So it wasn't burglary. My mind shied away from the implications of this observation and I looked at the papers on the desk. There was a large sheet of paper and a marker pen. On the paper Freda had written No Admittance in her careful script. Something more dreadful than even she had contemplated had occurred in the Museum Room, and no notice would have made any difference to that.

Chapter Nine

To my great relief, it was Roger Eliot who came. Watching from the window I saw him get out of the police car with a uniformed constable, whom he left unwinding the white tape with which the police mark the scene of a crime. I went to the front door to let him in.

"Hello, Sheila," he said. "What a dreadful thing. Did you find her?"

"No." Lionel Prentiss was at my elbow, pushing past me, almost brave now that the police had arrived and full of his own importance. "I found her. My name is Lionel Prentiss. I am a member of the committee. I let myself in with my key—members of the committee have keys, of course. I was going to make the punch for the concert tonight . . ."

He led the way along the passage, explaining as he went how he had found the body, how distressed he had been ("Freda Spencer was a truly remarkable person") and how (this said with an air of nonchalant bravery which made me smile) he had just been about to search the place for a possible intruder when I had arrived.

In the Museum Room Roger made a brief examination of the body and then looked around him. I could see him assessing the room, automatically checking the windows, looking for any sign of a struggle. He looked at me questioningly and I said, "Nothing gone, as far as I can see. In fact . . ."

Roger interrupted me. "Mr. Prentiss," he said, "you and Mrs. Malory have both had a dreadful shock. I wonder if you would mind making us all a cup of tea." Then, as Lionel Prentiss looked affronted at being assigned this menial domestic task, he went on, "I need a little time to evaluate the situation before I take your statement in full, and I think Mrs. Malory may be feeling a little faint."

I did my best to look frail—not a difficult task—and Lionel, now cast in the role of chivalrous protector, withdrew complacently into the kitchen. Roger shut the door.

"Right. Now then, Sheila, what were you going to tell me?"

"Just that it can't be burglary this time because her handbag's still there."

"I see."

"And there doesn't seem to be any sign of a forced entry here, or at the back."

"No." He was silent for a while and then he said, almost to himself, "Yes, of course, there was a burglary here a little while ago. I remember."

He moved over to the table and stood looking down at the notice and the uncapped marker pen lying beside it.

"Oh, the notice!" I said. "That was one of the reasons Freda was here this afternoon. That was part of the preparations for the concert this evening. She said there were several things she wanted to do."

"How many people would have known she'd be here?" Roger asked.

"Oh, quite a lot," I said. "Freda was a great one for letting everyone know just how much she did for Brunswick Lodge. We were all kept informed of her every movement. She told me at the coffee morning here today and I imagine pretty well everyone else in the room was aware of it."

"Your Mr. Prentiss had a key, but you didn't?"

"That's right. I'm not on the Committee, thank goodness. No, Freda said she'd let me in. I was bringing the canapés for this evening," I explained.

"Oh, I see. Was anyone else expected?"

"No, I don't think so. Well, not that I know of. Someone—probably Richard Lewis—would have been along early this evening to set out the chairs and get the room ready for the concert, but Freda liked to do most of the preparations herself."

"Mmm." Roger seemed lost in thought, staring down at the body.

"Roger."

He looked up. "Yes?"

"It was murder, then?"

"It looks like it. No weapon."

"What do you think it was? Some sort of knife?"

"I can't really say until I've had the path report, but, yes, I suppose it must have been." He looked round the room again. "Sheila, look, I know this is very distressing for you, but you know this place pretty well. Does anything look different—out of the ordinary?"

I tried to concentrate. The room looked very much as usual—apart, of course, from the still form lying beside the desk.

"I can't see anything . . . well, yes—the rope has been pushed to one side."

"The rope?"

"Freda insisted that we should have a rope rail—a rope attached to stands—in front of the exhibits on the walls, to stop the public getting too close and touching them. You see? That section at the far end has been pushed to one side."

Roger went over to look and I followed him.

"There." I made as if to straighten it and Roger stopped me.

"No, don't touch it."

I looked up at the wall and exclaimed, "The awl! It's gone!"

"The awl?"

"The cobbler's awl, one of the exhibits. It was part of the display—look, just here."

Roger went up close to look at the display. It was one of the Museum's most important exhibits, a set of eighteenth-century cobbler's tools: the awl, a metal last, a small hammer with a claw at one end, a special sort of knife for cutting the leather. These were all hung on a peg-board mount, beside a cured calfskin and an explanatory notice, making quite a large display that covered most of the wall at the far end of the room.

"What was it like?" Roger asked. "Can you describe it?"

"I can do better than that," I replied. "There's a picture of it in the catalogue. It was one of the really old things here, quite rare."

I flicked through the pages until I found the illustration. "There you are. That's it."

"It looks a vicious-looking thing," Roger said thoughtfully. "Quite capable of inflicting a wound."

He went back to the body (I found that if I kept thinking of the figure on the floor as "the body" I could somehow block from my mind the knowledge that it was Freda) and knelt beside it. "It will be pretty obvious when they do a proper examination," he said. "This awl thing seems to have been like a large, three-sided bodkin, so I imagine it would have made a triangular wound."

"There's no sign of it," I said, looking round in an ineffectual way.

Roger got to his feet. "I assume," he said, "that the murderer took it away."

"But why?" I asked, puzzled. "Whoever it was must have known that you'd realise quite soon what the murder weapon was."

"Yes, well," Roger moved towards the door, "I think we'll go and see what Mr. Prentiss is doing about the tea."

In the kitchen, Lionel was just putting some cups on a tray. "I couldn't find any milk," he said irritably, "and so I've had to open one of those long-life cartons from the cupboard. *Not* very satisfactory—it makes the tea *taste*."

"I'm sure it will be fine," I said placatingly. "It

was so good of you, Lionel. I really do feel the need for a cup! Shall I pour?"

I think we all felt better for a cup of tea. As Roger began to question Lionel, I moved tactfully away to the other end of the room. I didn't know if Roger wanted to ask me anything else and I thought I'd better be on hand in case he did.

I walked over and looked out of the window. Like the Museum Room, the kitchen was at the back of the building and looked out onto the garden. In the summer, thanks to several dedicated volunteers, the garden at Brunswick Lodge is bright with flowers and shrubs, a delightful setting for the many fêtes and garden parties held there. On this particular afternoon, though, with dusk falling, it was a melancholy sight. A strong wind was lashing the branches of the trees and whipping up the fallen leaves, then letting them fall in drifts across the wet flagstones. The terracotta planters alongside the house were empty now, the beds were bare of flowers and the soil looked cold and dank, as if nothing would ever grow in it again. I shuddered and turned back into the room.

Lionel was beginning to fuss. "We really must do something about the concert," he said. "People will be arriving in a few hours. The artists . . ."

"Yes, of course," I agreed. "Perhaps we should go into the office and start phoning people." I looked at Roger enquiringly. "Will that be all right?"

He nodded. "Yes. I'll just come with you and check that there's nothing in there that we should know about before you begin."

The office looked quite normal and I put my bag down on the desk and began to make a list of people for Lionel to telephone. Roger, pausing in the doorway, suddenly asked, "What about next of kin?"

"There's her daughter, Emily," I said. "She lives in Devon. I don't know her address, but Freda's cousin Olive will have it. Olive Clark? Have you come across her?"

"Oh yes, I know Miss Clark. She does Hospital Friends things with Jilly. Right. I'll get in touch with her. If you and Mr. Prentiss will contact as many people as you can. . . . The SOCO people will be along very soon to have a look at things in the Museum Room."

He went out of the room and Lionel and I settled to our task.

After a while I heard the doorbell ring and voices in the hall. I got up and went to see what was happening.

"Ah, Sheila," Roger said as he saw me, "I've

just been explaining to Mr. Lewis what has happened."

"Oh, Richard! I'm so sorry," I said. "We've just been trying to ring you but there was no reply."

Richard looked very pale and drawn but quite composed. "I've been for a walk," he said.

There was a pause. Somehow I couldn't bring myself to mention Freda's name. Then Lionel came out to see what was going on.

"Ah, Richard!" he exclaimed. "You've heard about Freda? Shocking thing. I found her, you know. Dreadful. *You* will be quite knocked up by it since she was such a friend of yours."

"Yes." Richard's mouth was set tight in a thin line, as if he couldn't trust himself to speak.

"Perhaps you'd lend us a hand," Lionel went on. "There's a great deal to do—everything to be canceled, people warned not to come this evening." He turned to me. "Some of the people who've come for the reunion; do you know which hotels they're staying at?"

"The Esplanade, I suppose, or the Anchor. Pam Nelson and her husband are at the Esplanade, I think, though of course she isn't Nelson any more. I don't know her married name."

"It's Watson." Richard's voice was not quite steady.

I turned to him and said, "Richard, there's no

need for you to stay. Lionel and I can manage perfectly well. Why don't you go home?"

"Yes," he said. "Yes, I think I will."

He went out of the room and again I heard the murmur of voices in the hall and then the slam of the front door as he went.

"Well, really, Sheila," Lionel protested, "we could have used another pair of hands."

"For goodness' sake, Lionel," I exclaimed impatiently, "couldn't you see how upset he was?"

"He seemed perfectly calm to me," Lionel said defensively. "In fact, I was surprised, really, after the way he's always carried on, mooning about around Freda all the time."

"He looked terrible," I said. "I just hope he's all right. Perhaps I shouldn't have let him go off on his own."

"Well, I certainly can't cope with all this by myself," Lionel said waspishly. "Did you manage to get hold of that pianist?"

"Yes, I've told all the musicians."

"I just hope we won't have to pay them. Their fees were going to come out of the ticket sales and now I suppose people will want their money back—though it's not *our* fault that the concert's had to be cancelled."

There was more noise and movement in the hall and when I looked out again I saw several figures, dressed in white, presumably the SOCO people that Roger had mentioned. I supposed they would take Freda away. I thought of those scenes in television dramas, the body in a zipped-up bag, a formless nothing. It seemed impossible to think in such a way of someone as positive as Freda.

"Well," Lionel said, "there's not much more we can do. There'll still be a lot of people turning up. Should we put some sort of notice on the door, 'Concert canceled owing to illness,' or something?"

"That would be understating it a bit," I said. "No. I expect Roger—Inspector Eliot—will leave a constable on duty. He'll tell people that it's all been canceled."

I picked up my handbag, preparing to go, and Lionel followed me out. "I'll just go and lock away the bottles of wine and that bottle of brandy," he said. "There is a cupboard in there with a key to it. Well," he went on, seeing my expression, "we don't want anyone taking it. It cost quite a bit."

He turned into the kitchen and I went in search of Roger. He was talking to one of the white-clad figures so I waited until he had finished before I approached him.

"Is it all right if I go now, Roger, or do you want me to make a statement?"

"Actually, I'd like you and Mr. Prentiss to give Sergeant Pope your statements now, while it's all fresh in your mind. Sorry about that. I know it's been pretty harrowing for you both, but if you could bear with us . . ."

Lionel emerged from the kitchen and Roger repeated his request.

"Perhaps you'd like to go first, Mr. Prentiss, since you actually found the body. The Sergeant is in that room on the right . . ."

"The Committee Room, yes, yes." Lionel bustled away.

Roger put his hand on my arm. "Are you all right, Sheila? Your Mr. Prentiss seems to be taking it all in his stride, but you look a bit done up. Will you be all right to drive yourself home?"

"Yes, I'm fine. It's just starting to sink in, I suppose. Oh, goodness!" I exclaimed. "What on earth am I to do with all those canapés?"

Roger smiled. "I'm sure you of all people will find a worthy cause to donate them to."

"Don't laugh," I said crossly. "It took ages to make them and I do *hate* waste. I know, I'll take them in to Inverdale, I know the matron there." Inverdale is an old people's home. "They can have them as an extra for supper."

Sergeant Pope was brisk and efficient and I was soon on my way down to Inverdale. Matron herself came to help me unload the canapés from the car.

"Well, it *is* kind of you, Mrs. Malory. It will make a nice change for my old people; they can have them with their high tea." She lifted the cling-film from one of the trays "Oh dear! I'm not sure about these anchovies. And what is this pink stuff?"

"Taramasalata," I said.

"I don't think taramasalata is really their cup of tea," Matron said obscurely. "But," she added, giving me a forgiving smile, "I became quite fond of it myself when my friend and I went on our trip to Corfu last year. We thought we'd like to go there because we both enjoyed those charming Gerald Durrell books so much. So perhaps I will save those for myself as a little treat."

I drove away from Inverdale strangely comforted by this exchange, feeling that I was once more back in the world I knew and could understand.

Chapter Ten

The next morning I tried to telephone Richard, but there was no reply. The ringing tone seemed to me to have that desolate quality of a phone unanswered and unheeded in an empty house.

"Surely he can't have gone out already," I said to Michael, who was piling the breakfast plates onto the draining board. "I do hope he's all right. He looked really terrible yesterday."

"Well, he would. After all, he's been devoted to Freda forever, poor sap. He must be absolutely gutted."

"Ye-es," I said doubtfully. "But it wasn't quite like that somehow. He seemed distressed but not actually unhappy, if you know what I mean."

"Not really."

"Well, very tense, as if he was holding back some really strong emotion, but I had the feeling somehow that it wasn't *grief*. Very odd."

"Well, if *he* isn't grieving for her, I can't imagine who will be," Michael said. "She could be pretty unpleasant. She was in the office last week to see Edward and he was late—he'd been to Colonel Welsh's funeral—and your chum Freda was really vile to Josie, as if it was *her* fault! Fortunately, Josie's pretty used to difficult clients, they go with the territory. But still!"

"Oh, I know. I suppose poor Olive will miss her and there's Laurence, of course. He'll miss her for quite other reasons, mostly financial." A sudden thought struck me. "I wonder if he knows? He was away yesterday, Freda told me, and wasn't expected back until late."

"I daresay someone will tell him. It doesn't take long for bad news to get around."

"That's true." I looked up from putting things into the dishwasher. "Shouldn't you be going? You'll be late."

"Oh Lord, is that the time? I've got a client at nine-thirty."

After Michael had gone, I rang Richard again, and again after I had made the beds. Still no reply. I found myself becoming increasingly uneasy, so much so that on my way in to do my shopping I made a detour and called at his flat.

Richard lives on the outskirts of Taviscombe in a large Victorian house which has been converted into three flats. Richard's is on the ground floor. I rang the bell, but there was no answer. The front of the house has been planted with shrubs which have now grown so big that it wouldn't have been possible to peer in through the windows even if I'd felt the inclination to do so. There was a side gate, though, but when I tried it, it was locked. I stood for a moment, hesitating, unsure of what to do, then I walked slowly back to my car.

I'd had to park a little way down the road because there were a couple of cars already parked outside the house. I didn't drive off straight away but sat for a while, wondering what, if anything, I ought to do about Richard. His manner had been so odd, not just yesterday, which would have been understandable, but over the whole of the last few days, so that I was especially concerned about him.

My thoughts were interrupted by the sight of someone coming out of the driveway of Richard's flats. It was Pamela Nelson. She got into one of the cars parked outside and drove away.

For the rest of the day I wondered and speculated. What could have changed Richard's attitude to Freda so drastically? What did Pam Nelson have to do with it? And what, if anything, did it have to do with Freda's murder?

* * *

I saw Laurence Marvell the following day. It was the sort of miserable morning when the sky is an unrelenting iron-grey and the wind is bitter and seems to go right through you however warmly you think you have dressed, and every breath you take is sharp and painful in your nostrils. I was in Boots buying the vitamin C tablets with which I fondly hope to keep winter colds at bay, when I met Laurence. As I greeted him I thought how dreadful he looked; his face was pale and pinched-looking and there were shadows under his eyes, as if he hadn't slept.

"Ah, Sheila," he said with an attempt at his usual suave manner. "How are you on this horrible day?"

We exchanged commonplaces about the weather until we had both been served and then I said, "I'm so very sorry about Freda—such an awful thing. It must have been a dreadful shock to you. You were away, weren't you?"

"I got back quite late," he said. "Look, we can't talk here. Come over to the Buttery and have a coffee."

In the warmth of the Buttery with a cup of coffee before him, Laurence looked a little better, though still not himself.

"I was away in London," he said, "and didn't

get back until late—ten-o'clockish. Then the next morning, quite early, about eight I should think, I had a phone call from Richard . . ."

"From Richard!" I exclaimed.

"Yes. Telling me . . . it was very odd. He just said, 'Freda's been murdered,' and rang off."

"How extraordinary!"

"I didn't believe it at first. I thought—well, I don't know what I thought—that Richard had gone off his head, I suppose. Anyway, I thought I'd better ask *someone* if it was true, so I phoned Olive and she said that it was. She sounded a bit peculiar too—quite naturally, of course, they were very close—so I didn't press her for details. I don't suppose *you* know any more?"

"Well, yes, as a matter of fact, I do. I was there, at Brunswick Lodge, just after she was found." I told Laurence briefly what had happened and he listened in silence.

When I had finished he said, "I still can't believe it. Freddie dead. It's just not possible! And murder! I mean, who on earth would have wanted to kill her, and why?"

I didn't say anything and he went on, "I know she could be difficult and she upset people, but, well, you don't *murder* someone for that sort of thing."

"No," I said, "not for that sort of thing."

"Perhaps it was robbery," he suggested. "There was that other time."

"Nothing was taken," I said, "and there was no sign of any sort of break-in."

He shook his head. "It just doesn't seem real. Murder . . ." He drank the last of his coffee.

"You will miss her," I said.

"Miss her?" He looked at me blankly for a moment and then said, "Yes, I'll miss her. She was very much a part of my life."

I was struck, as I had been with Richard, at the almost mechanical response, the lack of grief in his voice.

"I must be going," I said. "Thank you for the coffee." I pulled on my gloves. "I hope your aunt is well."

"My aunt?"

"In London."

"Oh, my aunt. Yes, she's much better now." He got up from the table. "Thank you, Sheila, for telling me all about it. I hope," he added with a brief return to his old smooth manner, "that it wasn't too painful for you to go over it like this. It must have been a dreadful shock for you, seeing her like that."

"Yes, it was."

"I suppose Olive will be making all the

arrangements for the funeral, and so on? Or her daughter?"

"I suppose so," I said. "Though I don't know when the police will release the body. There'll have to be an inquest, of course."

"Yes, of course," he said thoughtfully. "That will hold everything up."

"I mean," I said to Rosemary when I called round there later that day, "he seemed upset, just as Richard did, but not *sad* upset, if you know what I mean."

"Well, far be it from me to speak ill of the dead," Rosemary said. "No, that's not true, there are several people I could speak ill of dead or alive, and, actually, Freda is one of them. Honestly, who is going to grieve for her? Especially if, as you say, Richard doesn't. That really *is* peculiar!"

"Something happened the night of the reunion dinner," I said. "I'm sure of it. Something to do with Pam Nelson." I told her about Pam's visit to Richard earlier in the day.

"Do you think there is some sort of connection with Freda's murder?" Rosemary suggested. "No! There couldn't be—not Richard. He's adored her for years!"

"But she treated him abominably," I said, "and

I think he'd really reached breaking-point." Feeling a bit as if I was betraying a confidence, though Richard had never asked for my silence, I described Richard's outburst after the attack on Freda at Brunswick Lodge.

" 'If she dies I shall be free. I hope she dies.' That's what he said."

"Oh, but he was upset," Rosemary protested, "distraught about the attack. People say all sorts of things in those circumstances."

"He was pretty well on the edge," I said. "I don't think it would have taken much to push him over. Perhaps the thing with Pam Nelson—whatever that might have been—was all it took."

"But Richard is such a mild, inoffensive creature!"

"He is now," I said, "after all these years of being ground down by Freda. But he wasn't always like that. Remember what he was like when we were young?"

Rosemary was silent for a moment. "Yes, you're right," she said. "He was quite different then. You forget, don't you, when you see people nearly every day, what they used to be like."

"Some people improve with age, some don't. Though I think that, in the end, we get *more* like our selves as we get older, if you see what I mean."

"Well, Mother certainly has," Rosemary said bitterly. "Guess what! she's gone and upset Miss Marshall. She was really rude about Miss Marshall's sister—you know, the one who got the MBE—and the poor soul is so proud of her and was deeply offended. So now she doesn't call any more. Mother never can keep a friend for long, and then when she's all alone—entirely her own fault, because of that wicked tongue of hers—she expects *me* to be round there all the time."

"Poor you!" I said sympathetically. "It isn't fair."

"Who said life's fair?" Rosemary said. "Oh yes, I knew there was something I wanted to ask you. Can you give me a hand tomorrow to sort out those things we've collected for the Romanians? The lorry's calling at Brunswick Lodge at the end of the week to pick them up. Roger says his people have finished there, so we can use it—everywhere except the Museum Room, which is still locked."

"Sure," I said. "What time?"

"Oh, about ten-thirty, if that's all right with you. It shouldn't take long with two of us."

The next day the wind had dropped and the sun, although weak and wintry, lifted one's spirits. However, as I got out of my car at Brunswick

Lodge, I felt reluctant to go in. The memory of Freda's body lying on the floor was very vivid, but I braced myself, opened the door, and went in. Once inside it wasn't so bad.

Rosemary called from the kitchen, "Is that you, Sheila? I'm in here."

The kitchen was warm, there was steam coming from the kettle and two cups and a jar of coffee were laid out comfortingly on the worktop. "I got Mr. Soames—in a good mood for once—to bring all the stuff down from where Sybil had stored it upstairs, because I thought it would be cosier to do it down here. I've got masses of cardboard boxes, so if we put the clothes in these and all the babies' stuff in these and the tins in *these* and label them, then they can just be loaded up on the lorry out at the back."

"Splendid!" I said, moving over to the pile of tinned food by the window to make a start. I looked out and to my surprise saw Rosemary's granddaughter, Delia, a cheerful little figure in a bright pink anorak and a woolly hat, digging in one of the flowerbeds. "Good gracious, is that Delia?"

"Yes. I said I'd have her while Jilly went to the dentist. Alex is at play school, but Delia's school has the day off today—some sort of staff training thing. It really is extraordinary the way they never seem to *be* at school these days. A whole week off for half-term as well, can you believe it?"

"How's she liking school?" I asked. "This is only her first term, isn't it?"

"Well," Rosemary said, stuffing a pile of miscellaneous woollen garments into one of the boxes, "it's early days yet. The novelty and the excitement over her school uniform haven't worn off yet. But no tears or anything, thank goodness. I think she'll be warm enough out there, she's well wrapped up and I thought it would get her out from under our feet. She's going through a *gardening* phase at the moment. Jilly gave her her own bit of garden and she had a children's trowel and fork set for her birthday, so she's been digging things up ever since. I don't think she can do any damage there. The gardeners haven't started to plant that bed yet."

We bent to our task and were just about finishing when Sybil came in.

"There now!" she said. "I meant to be here to give you a hand, but Pauline held me up. She couldn't find her car keys *again*! I'm sorry."

"Never mind," Rosemary said cheerfully. "You can make the coffee. The kettle has boiled once; it'll only need warming up."

Sybil took off her coat and laid it across the back of a chair.

"Better hang it up," I said warningly. "Otherwise it might get packed with all this stuff."

"I wasn't sure if we'd be able to get in here today," Sybil said, spooning coffee into the mugs. "I mean, I wondered if the police would have finished."

"No, it's only the Museum Room itself that's still locked up," I said. I straightened up and rubbed my aching back. "There, that's done. No, I don't think they're particularly interested in the rest of the Lodge."

"You were here when the body was discovered, weren't you?" Sybil asked. "That must have been pretty dreadful."

"I arrived just after Lionel had found her," I said. "It *was* awful. But in a sort of way, unreal. You know, you keep saying to yourself that this can't be happening . . ."

"Well," Sybil said in her usual brusque manner, "I'm not going to be hypocritical enough to say that I shall grieve for her. I thoroughly disliked her and I think a lot of people will be happier now that she's gone. But I do draw the line at murder."

"It does seem extraordinary to think that she's gone," Rosemary said. "Especially here. I keep half expecting her to come in through that door and tell us that we're doing this all wrong."

"I know what you mean," I agreed. "If Freda's ghost is going to walk anywhere, it will surely be at Brunswick Lodge."

"How's Laurence taking it?" Sybil asked. "*He'll* miss her!"

"He looked terrible when I saw him," I said. "Very upset, but not, as I told Rosemary, unhappy-upset, if you know what I mean, more put out."

"I'm not surprised." Sybil gave a contemptuous snort. "There's his meal-ticket gone."

"Ye-es," I agreed. "But there was something else, I can't quite pin it down. It was almost as if he was disconcerted."

"Well, you would be, wouldn't you," Sybil demanded, "if your cash flow dried up."

"You don't think he cared for her at all?" Rosemary asked.

"I think he was flattered at all the attention she paid him," I said. "And there's the money thing, too. Well, we don't know if it was actual *money,* do we, or just clothes and holidays and expensive little treats. But she *was* supposed to be a friend and he didn't seem to be mourning her as a friend."

"What about the funeral?" Sybil asked as we drank our coffee.

"I don't know." I turned to Rosemary. "Has Roger said anything to you or Jack about when the inquest will be?"

"No, but I imagine it will be quite soon."

"Gran?" A small figure came in through the garden door. "Gran, I'm hungry. Can I have a biscuit?"

Rosemary reached into the cupboard and brought out a tin. "Does anyone else want one?" she asked.

Sybil and I shook our heads.

"I dug up the whole flowerbed," Delia said, her voice slightly muffled by biscuit, "but there was nothing to plant so I put some twigs in and they *might* grow into trees. Gran, will you come out and look at my twigs?"

"Not now, darling," Rosemary said, gathering up a few odds and ends stuffing them into her shopping bag. "We've got to get back, Mummy will be waiting for us."

Delia came over to me. "*I've* got a handbag," she said, displaying what I recognised as an old black suede shoulder bag of Rosemary's.

"Isn't that nice?" I said admiringly. "You do look grown up."

"Shall I show you what I've got in my bag?" Delia offered.

"Come along, darling," Rosemary called. "We must hurry now."

"I'll see it another time," I said. "You mustn't keep Gran waiting."

Delia seemed about to protest, but Rosemary said placatingly, "It's sausage and chips for lunch. And ice cream for afters," and with a wave to us she hustled Delia away.

"That child is getting thoroughly spoilt," Sybil said disapprovingly.

"Oh well," I said, "it's a grandparent's privilege! I just wish I had a grandchild to spoil."

Sybil washed up the cups and I put them away.

"What *about* the funeral, then?" she asked.

"What about it?"

"Who will represent Brunswick Lodge?" Sybil said impatiently.

"Oh, goodness, I don't know. I expect people will just go individually, as it were."

"I suppose so." Sybil looked dissatisfied. Then, brightening up, she said, "I shall start making a collection tomorrow for a funeral wreath from the committee."

Chapter Eleven

The inquest was only a formality, really. The police asked for an adjournment and Freda's funeral was arranged for the following Thursday.

"Ma," Michael said, handing me a bit of crumpled black cloth, "can you do anything with this? It seems to have got a bit chewed up and I really ought to wear it, because Edward asked me to represent the firm at Freda Spencer's funeral."

"Oh, darling, I *wish* you'd told me before. You really need a new black tie and it's too late to get you one now, with the funeral tomorrow. I suppose I'll just have to see what I can do with an iron and a damp cloth."

The church was almost full, thank goodness. Most of the Committee from Brunswick Lodge were there and people representing various other organisations that Freda had belonged to. I looked around for other familiar faces. Roger was sitting beside Rosemary and her husband, Jack, though whether in his official capacity or simply as an acquaintance I didn't know. Laurence Marvell was near the front, as were Sybil and Pauline, but I couldn't see any sign of Richard.

There was a slight stir and we all turned to watch the coffin as it was carried in, followed by Olive and Emily as the chief mourners. I hadn't seen Emily for several years and I was shocked to see how she had aged. Even allowing for the distress natural on such an occasion, she looked exceptionally pale and haggard. As they passed up the aisle I saw Olive put her arm protectively round her shoulder and Emily gave her a flicker of a smile.

After the service at the cemetery, when the grim formalities were over, Olive said, "Will you and Michael come back to the house—just for a sandwich and a glass of sherry?"

"Yes, of course."

"I've only invited a few people," Olive said confidentially. "I don't think Emily can face a crowd, but it would be nice if just a few friends—well, you know . . ."

Olive still lived in her parents' house on West Hill. It was a large, rather gloomy place, set back from the road, the short drive lined with the drearier kind of evergreen. There was a Gothic-looking high-pitched roof and Victorian stained glass in the front door. It was, of course, far too large for Olive, but she had stubbornly refused to move into the bungalow or the nice little flat that well-wishers had suggested, saying only that she didn't think Tinker would like it.

"Besides," she added, "Emily might want to come back to Taviscombe one day and it would be nice for her to have somewhere with a bit of space for the children."

Fortunately, Olive had enough money, even in this day and age, to pay for the upkeep of a large house and for a daily woman and a weekly gardener.

When we arrived, Sybil and Pauline were already there, talking to Emily, who seemed a little overwhelmed by Sybil's brisk manner.

"Oh, Sheila, and Michael dear, come in and get warm," Olive greeted us. "It really is quite bitter out. Now do help yourselves to sandwiches—Mrs. Newsome came in this morning specially to make them—and a glass of sherry. Unless you'd rather have whisky, Michael? I know Papa always said that sherry was a ladies' drink. There, is that all right?"

Then, as I went over to stroke the large tabby cat sitting complacently in an armchair by the fire, who acknowledged my greeting with a rusty purr, she went on, "There now, I'm sure Tinker remembers you. Who's a clever boy, then!"

Sybil broke away from Emily and moved towards the door. "Sorry to dash," she said, "but we really must be going."

"Oh dear, must you?" Olive asked. "You've only just arrived."

"Yes," Sybil said. "Sorry about that. We only looked in to pay our respects; we've got to be at the Forsyths' in Milverton for lunch. Nice to have seen you again, Emily. Sorry not to have a chat, Sheila. Come along, Pauline!" and she swept her sister out of the room.

"I'll just see you out," Olive said. "And you two come and have a word with Emily. Emily, dear, you remember Sheila Malory and her son Michael, don't you?"

Seen close up, Emily looked even more careworn. Her dark eyes seemed enormous in her pale face and her hair was dull and lifeless and chopped about, as if she had cut it herself. She was wearing a beige jumper and a rather too long brown skirt which made her look even more colourless.

She gave me her shy, sideways smile that I remembered from years ago, and said, "Yes, of course I remember Mrs. Malory, and Michael, too."

"It's *so* nice to see you again, Emily," I began in the overeffusive manner I find I use in slightly difficult situations. "Though I'm sorry it's on such a sad occasion. How are the children?"

"They're fine. Ben's looking after them. It's term time, so I didn't want to take them out of school. Anyway, I don't think children should go to funerals and it's not as though they ever *knew* their grandmother, and Ben certainly wouldn't have come. I mean, it would have been hypocritical, wouldn't it? She always hated him. I'm only here myself because of Olive—I didn't want her to have to cope with everything. Mummy was a horrible person, she was foul to me and tried to ruin my life, and I can't possibly say that I'm sorry she's dead."

All this came out in a great rush and I was rather taken aback, holding, I suppose, the conventional view that one shouldn't speak ill of the dead immediately after the funeral.

Emily saw my surprise and said, with a faint smile, "I'm sorry, I've shocked you. But after living with Ben all these years, I find I can say what I think and not what people expect me to say. I had enough of that when I was young. You know what Mummy was like."

"Yes," I said, "I do. And I'm not shocked, really. I do understand how things were."

Emily finished her sherry and bent to put the glass down on a small brass table. "It wasn't so bad when Daddy was alive," she said. "But after, well, I don't know what I'd have done if I hadn't met Ben."

"How is the smallholding going?" I asked.

She shrugged. "It's not easy," she said, "but we manage. And now that Mummy's dead we should be able to afford to expand and buy new equipment."

There was a short silence. I found the fact that Emily hadn't mentioned the way her mother had died embarrassing, and didn't know what to say.

But Michael, who had been standing beside me silently listening to this conversation, was bolder and said, "It must have been a dreadful shock to hear about her death. I mean, murder is always disturbing, and when it's someone close . . ."

She was silent a moment and then said thoughtfully, "Yes, I suppose so. But, to be honest, I was so glad she was dead that I didn't really care how it happened." She turned to me and said, "There now, that really *is* shocking, isn't it? But she's been such a monster in my life. I've always been afraid of her, I suppose, and felt that, even though I'd got away and had my own life with Ben and the children, she'd somehow manage to spoil it for me, like she spoilt everything when I was young. But I'm free now."

I thought of Richard and his reaction when he thought Freda was dead after the burglary.

"It's wonderful to feel free at last," Emily repeated.

"God moves in a mysterious way," said a voice behind me. It was Olive. "Do have another sandwich," she went on, holding out a plate. "Come along, Michael, I'm sure you can manage another one."

"How long are you staying in Taviscombe?" I asked Emily, trying to get the conversation back onto a more commonplace level.

"Oh, just a few days. There are a couple of legal matters to be cleared up." She turned to Michael. "Please tell Mr. Drayton that I'll be in to see him on Monday. Then I must go home and," she said, smiling affectionately at her, "Olive is coming with me."

"Yes," Olive said, beaming. "Won't that be nice?"

"It's a bit of a squash," Emily said, laughing, "but we manage to fit her in somehow."

"I'm really looking forward to it." Olive turned to me. "Betty Slade from next door will look after Tinker, of course; otherwise I couldn't possibly leave him."

* * *

"The whole thing was really weird," Michael said as we got into the car and drove home. "I mean, Freda Spencer was *murdered*, dammit, and they simply didn't mention it."

"I know," I agreed. "It was very odd. I know Olive's getting very vague now, and I do see that Emily has no reason to mourn her mother, but still, you'd have thought they'd have said *something*! If you hadn't brought it up—and I do think it was brave of you—nothing would have been said at all."

"It's almost as if they'd wiped the murder from their minds," Michael said thoughtfully. "If they didn't talk about it, then it didn't exist."

"I can see that Emily mightn't feel much grief at her mother's death, there was no love lost there, on either side. But Olive was very close to Freda. At least, she used to be before Freda took up with Laurence Marvell. You'd think *she'd* have said something about the murder."

"Actually," Michael said, "I think Olive's so chuffed at having Emily to stay with her that she hasn't given Freda's murder a thought."

"Bless her," I said. "You may be right; she really does dote on Emily and the children, and I know she's been unhappy that Emily would never come and stay in Taviscombe in case she ran into Freda. Anyway," I continued, "Emily and Ben will be able to make a real go of that smallholding now. I imagine Freda will have left her quite a tidy sum. I know Bill left Emily a reasonable legacy, but he was a very rich man and Freda was quite shrewd about money in her own right . . ."

"Oh yes," Michael agreed, "there's a fair bit of dosh. But, well, I suppose I really oughtn't to tell you this—client confidentiality and all that—but the police know about it, they've been making enquiries."

"The police?"

"Yes, well, you remember I told you that Freda had been in to see Edward just before she died?"

"When she was so beastly to Josie? Yes."

"She came in to alter her will."

"What?" I took my eyes off the road momentarily to stare unbelievingly at Michael, causing the car to swerve.

"Steady, Ma," he said urgently, "you'll have us in the ditch!"

"You shouldn't tell me startling things like that when I'm driving. So who did Freda leave her money to, then?"

"Well, after a few legacies to charities and so on, and some bits of furniture to Olive, she told

Edward she wanted to leave the whole lot to Laurence Marvell."

"Good God! And nothing for Emily?"

"Nothing at all."

"Oh, poor Emily," I cried. "How awful for her! I mean, not just for what they could do with the money—and I'd say they really need it just now—but to feel that her mother hated her so much. And really, it was Bill's money, after all. He would have been horrified! To think of that slimy Laurence Marvell getting his greedy hands on the lot. It's a tragedy!"

"Well, actually," Michael said, "it's not."

"What?"

"Freda came in to give Edward her instructions about the new will, but although it was drawn up, she died before she could sign it, so it's invalid."

"She was murdered before she could sign it," I corrected him. "Well now, I wonder who knew about the new will?"

"Considering the plans she was making so confidently today, it's fairly obvious that Emily didn't."

"But," I broke in, "I bet Laurence did. Freda couldn't have resisted telling him. It would be the surest way of keeping her hold over him. Oh well," I concluded with some satisfaction, "*he'll* be disappointed at any rate. It was perfectly obvious that was the main reason he hung around Freda—I mean, he knew she didn't get on with Emily. I just wish I could see his face when he finds out about the will."

I let the dogs out into the garden and gave Foss, who was sitting on the worktop doing his usual impersonation of an ill-treated, abandoned, starving animal, his fifth meal of the day.

"Do you want anything to eat?" I asked Michael. "I imagine you've got time for a snack before you go back to work. Or did you eat enough of Olive's sandwiches?"

"I am a bit peckish," he said. "Funeral baked meats aren't really filling. I mean, you don't feel you can eat the lot."

"How about cheese on toast?" I suggested. "You put the coffee on while I grate the cheese."

As I busied myself with the cheese and bread I said, "A pretty good motive for murder, wouldn't you say?"

"*Two* pretty good motives, if you come to think of it," Michael said. "Both Emily *and* Laurence Whatsit, each thinking they were going to get all that lovely money."

"Exactly. You say the police know about the will? So I suppose Roger will be investigating their alibis. I know he says he always looks for a financial motive first."

"As I said, there's a lot of money involved."

"Laurence Marvell was supposed to be in London," I said. "He told me he didn't get back until late—ten o'clock, I think it was—but he could just have said that." I put the slices of bread and cheese under the grill. "I suppose Emily might have an alibi down in North Devon. How frustrating not to know!"

"But surely," Michael protested, "it *couldn't* have been Emily. I mean, how on earth could she have known that Freda would be at Brunswick Lodge at that particular time?"

"I don't know," I replied. "Olive might have said something—they talk to each other a lot on the phone. And she might just have come up to Taviscombe . . ."

"On the off-chance of getting an opportunity to murder her mother!" Michael laughed. "Come off it, Ma!"

"Yes, well, I agree it does sound a little farfetched, but there might be *some* way she could have known." I slid the toasted cheese onto a plate and put it in front of him. "Here, eat up your nice food and stop putting obstacles in the way of a perfectly good theory."

"You don't honestly believe that Emily could actually have killed her mother, do you?"

"You can never tell. I know she looks a wispy little thing, but her family and that smallholding mean an awful lot to her, and if she thought she might be going to lose it all . . . I'm sure she was counting on Freda's money. So either she thought she was going to inherit and killed Freda because they needed the money badly *now,* or else she somehow heard that Freda was thinking of changing her will and decided to kill her quickly before she did!"

"But how *could* she have known?" Michael demanded.

"I wouldn't have put it past Freda to have told her. I know they weren't really speaking to each other, but say Emily was absolutely desperate for money and, as a really last resort, appealed to her mother—after all, the money was Bill's and Emily might quite reasonably have assumed she'd be left at least some of it. But if Freda had refused and there was a row, then I could easily imagine her *enjoying* telling Emily that she was changing her will and leaving the lot to Laurence."

"You may be right about that, but I still think it's all a bit improbable. Perhaps you'd better concentrate on the Laurence Marvell aspect."

"I wonder if he knows yet that Freda hadn't signed the new will?"

"There's no reason why he should."

"No, but he'd have expected by now to have been told if she *had* left him everything. I mean, now the funeral's over and all that. He hasn't made any enquiries, has he?"

"Not that I know of, but then he hardly could."

"No, I suppose not. Oh well, perhaps I'll manage to contrive some way of bumping into him to see what I can find out."

Michael smiled at me affectionately. "I expect you will, Ma," he said.

Chapter Twelve

I didn't have to do much contriving, though, because a few days later I had a session with my dentist at twelve and then a hairdressing appointment at two. It hardly seemed worth going all the way home, so I dropped into the pub by the harbour for a sandwich and a drink and found myself face to face with Laurence Marvell, sitting at the same table we had sat at when he and Freda and I had had lunch there that day before Christmas. He was not alone. Sitting with him was a youngish man, small and slight with improbably fair hair and wearing black jeans, an open-necked black shirt, and a pale beige suede jacket.

I paused hopefully beside their table. "Hello, Laurence," I said brightly. "Fancy seeing you here!"

I put my plate of sandwiches and glass down on the table while I fastened my handbag, so that he was obliged to say (rather grudgingly), "Won't you join us?"

"Well," I said, sitting down quickly, "if you're sure I'm not interrupting. It's nice and warm in here. The wind blowing in from the sea is always so fierce."

I looked enquiringly at his companion and Laurence said, "This is my friend James Webster. James, this is Sheila Malory, one of Freddie's friends."

The man held out his hand. "Call me Jimmy," he said.

So this was the Jimmy we all thought Laurence no longer saw. I wondered if Freda had known that the affair was still going on. I was pretty sure she hadn't.

"How nice to meet you," I replied, shaking hands. "Laurence said you were in the theatre. Are you an actor?"

Jimmy gave a burst of shrill laughter, so that the people at the next table turned and stared at him. "Goodness, *no*!" he exclaimed. "That's not *me*, now is it, Larry! No, I'm in the wardrobe at Covent Garden."

"Oh, really," I said uncertainly. "That sounds very glamorous."

"Oh *no*, Sheila. You don't mind if I call you

Sheila? That's what people always say when I tell them, but it's really *very* hard work!"

"Yes, I suppose it must be. Some of those opera costumes are very elaborate . . ."

"Oh my dear, don't tell me! That second act change of Violetta's! So heavy. How the poor cow bears it I do not know! Absolute *death* to iron."

"Really!"

"Mind you, the ballet's even worse. Do you know how many layers of tulle there are in a tutu? Repairing *them* is no joke, I can tell you. Not to mention the laundry, back and forth to the cleaners, dear, after every performance. It's the perspiration, you see." He leaned forward confidentially. "It rots the fabric in no time if you don't keep a *very* beady eye!"

"Goodness!" I said, fascinated by this glimpse of the more mundane side of backstage life.

"Yes, well," Laurence interrupted, "I don't suppose Sheila wants to hear about all that."

"Oh, no," I said, "I think it's absolutely riveting!"

Jimmy seemed inclined to expatiate on the problems he encountered but Laurence said, "Is Emily staying in Taviscombe for long?"

"No," I replied. "Just to clear up things with the lawyers. Then she and Olive are going back to Devon."

Jimmy gave his friend a sharp look and opened his mouth as if to say something, but Laurence said hastily, "I didn't introduce myself at the funeral. It hardly seemed a suitable moment."

"No," I said, "I suppose not. Actually, I haven't seen her myself for years. As you know, she and Freda didn't get on so she never came to Taviscombe. And, of course, she has a large family and then there's the smallholding. Both she and Ben (that's her husband) work very hard. Mind you," I said casually, "life will be very much easier for them now that there's going to be quite a bit more money."

Laurence gave me a hard stare and then dropped his eyes.

I turned to Jimmy. "Are you staying long in Taviscombe?" I asked.

"Well, I've got a bit of holiday due," he replied. "It's quieter you know, now the repertoire's settled down after Christmas. And I can certainly do with a bit of a rest, I can tell you, after that new production of *Rheingold*. What a carry-on that was!"

"Oh yes," I said. "I read about that in the papers."

"You wouldn't *believe* how difficult all that silver lamé is to sew—frays at the edges soon as you *look* at it, dear. No, I was ever so glad to get away for a bit. Oh, the *rows*, dear, between the designer and the producer. And who has to make it all work, I ask you? Us, the poor bloody infantry. Such a *business*—fuss, fuss, fuss! Marie, she's head of wardrobe, and she got *really*—well, I don't like to say it!" He leaned towards me and mouthed, "Hormones, dear. Well, it's her age, isn't it? But honestly, it was like living in a madhouse! I said to Terry—he's one of the dressers, such a sweet boy—I said, 'If that woman speaks to me again like that I shall *resign*. I shall, really.' I mean, I've got my feelings and, honestly, Madam could have given Hitler a few lessons that week before the dress rehearsal!"

"How awful!"

"So when I heard from poor Larry here that this awful thing had happened, I thought I really ought to come down and *support* him. Well, what are friends *for*, I ask you?"

"Did you ever meet Freda?" I asked.

"Only the once. Larry brought her to Derek's party after that thing at the Royal Court. She seemed a very nice lady."

Laurence made no comment on this unusual summary of Freda's character and neither did I.

"It was a dreadful shock to us all," I said. "Murder is a terrible thing, and when it's someone you actually know . . ."

"Oh, I *know,* dear. I remember when poor Ronnie had that ghastly accident—he fell from the flies halfway through the lighting rehearsal of *Tosca* and died instantly. Mind you, we never really believed that it *was* an accident. He was a very highly strung boy, and he'd had that *dreadful* row with Jason . . ."

Laurence broke in. "Sorry to interrupt, but I'm afraid we have to go." I looked at my watch and exclaimed regretfully, "Goodness, so must I! I ought to be at the hairdresser's in five minutes."

I finished off the rest of my gin and tonic and said, "It's been so nice seeing you both. Perhaps," I turned to Jimmy, "we may meet again before you go back to London?"

Laurence gave an unconvincing smile and said, "Yes, that would be lovely," and hustled Jimmy out.

"*Very* camp," I said to Michael that evening, "but very cosy. And I must say I long to hear more about life backstage!"

"I thought that particular relationship was supposed to be over," Michael said.

"I'm pretty sure that's what Freda thought, but obviously not. All those times he was going up to London to see his aunt—I never quite believed in *that*! Have I put salt in this cauliflower, did you notice? Oh, never mind. I'll put a bit more in for luck. I suppose Jimmy came rushing down to see if Laurence *did* inherit Freda's money. *What* a disappointment for them both!"

"Emily came in today to see Edward about getting probate and everything," Michael said.

"Did he say anything to her about Freda changing her will?" I asked curiously.

"I don't know. Probably not. I mean, why upset her for nothing? And it's not likely that Laurence will contest it or anything."

"Now there's a thought!"

"No, not likely. The expense and general hoo-ha would put him off, especially since Emily is Freda's daughter and *she* could probably accuse him of undue influence."

"Well, it does mean that, if we eliminate Emily (and really I don't see how she *could* have done it), Laurence has a pretty strong motive, especially since we now know that Jimmy is still on the scene."

"You'll have to see if you can ask Roger about his alibi."

"Yes, well, I'll certainly try." I drained the potatoes and started to mash them.

"Ma," Michael said suddenly, "is your hair *meant* to be that colour?"

I groaned. "Oh dear, I did hope that the mirror

was lying! Karen persuaded me to have a rinse to brighten it up. I knew it was a mistake! Oh well," I said, more in hope than expectation, "perhaps it will wash out."

That weekend Michael was away and, as I woke up early, I thought I'd go and get the Sunday paper and take the dogs for a walk along the beach. It was a greyish sort of morning with a brisk wind blowing and a hint of rain in the air. The dogs are both getting old now, especially Tessa, but on the beach they always seem to become rejuvenated and rush about, splashing through pools and barking madly at seagulls. I walked with them, enjoying the fresh morning air, and watching with pleasure the waves creaming into the shore and the white horses on the sea out beyond the harbour.

The rain was definitely falling now so I rounded up the dogs and shut them in the back of the car (resolutely ignoring the wet sand and bits of seaweed they brought with them) and was just about to get in myself when I saw a familiar figure, in an unfamiliar guise, trotting along beside the sea wall.

"Hello, Roger," I called out as he approached. "Don't tell me you've taken up jogging!"

He leaned on the wall while he got his breath

back. "It's Jilly, really, she's worried about my lifestyle. She says I don't get enough exercise. She wanted me to go to the gym at the Westwood, but I didn't think I could face that. The jogging is a compromise."

"Look, come into the car," I said. "This rain is freezing! I think there's a bit of hail falling, too. Getting pneumonia is not the way to keep fit."

The dogs, behind their wire mesh at the back, gave Roger a vociferous welcome as he got in.

"Yes, you're right, Sheila," he said, drying his hair with a handkerchief. "It's a bit too cold for me!"

"Do you have to get back straight away?" I asked. "Or have you got a spare moment?"

"No, I don't need to be anywhere before midday today. What is it?"

"I just wondered how it's going? The case, I mean. Are you any further forward? Did you find the weapon?"

"No. I don't suppose we will, now. We searched pretty thoroughly in Brunswick Lodge, but there was no sign. It could have been thrown into the sea or buried somewhere, there are endless possibilities. Anyway, it probably wouldn't have told us a great deal. I imagine the murderer wore gloves or wiped it clean."

"I suppose so. How about people's alibis?"

"We're still checking. But Emily, that's the daughter, seems to be in the clear. She was seen by a couple of independent witnesses miles away in North Devon at the time the murder was committed. I know she had the strongest motive—money usually is—but really, it wasn't very probable that she'd have known exactly where her mother was likely to be at a specific time. A pity, but there it is."

I wiped some of the condensation away from the windscreen with my glove. "There was someone else, who had expectations," I said. "I expect you know that."

Roger gave me a quizzical look. "Michael has been talking, has he? You mean Laurence Marvell, I suppose? Yes, we are aware of that particular situation."

"You mustn't think Michael has been indiscreet," I said hastily. "Well, perhaps he has, but only to me and I certainly haven't told anyone. But I did see Laurence the day before yesterday and he wasn't alone." I explained about my meeting in the pub.

Roger laughed. "Oh, you've met the egregious Jimmy, have you? Quite a colourful character!"

"Yes, but I'm sure Freda had no idea *that* affair was still going on. Laurence used to tell her that he was going up to London to see his aunt. I'm positive he was only interested in Freda's money and, if he thought she was going to leave it to him . . ."

"You think she would have told him?" Roger asked.

"Oh yes!" I said emphatically. "That's *just* what she would have done to keep him attentive."

"He says he was driving back from London the day she was killed, and that he didn't get back to Taviscombe until late. Not an easy alibi to check, but difficult to disprove, unless someone actually saw him in Taviscombe before he said he was."

"Of course," I said thoughtfully, "Laurence could easily have made those two other attempts on Freda."

"Two attempts?" Roger looked at me sharply.

"Well, yes," I said. "If you come to think of it, this murder might be third time lucky. At least," I caught myself up, "third time *unlucky* for poor Freda!"

"I knew about the break-in when she was hit on the head at Brunswick Lodge, of course," Roger said. "We did investigate that. But I didn't know that there had been another incident. What happened?"

I told him about Freda's near escape in the steam room at the Westwood and he looked serious.

"I see what you mean," he said slowly. "It does

seem more than a coincidence, certainly. Can you let me have the times and a detailed statement about this steam room business? I can see that I have a lot more checking to do. Laurence Marvell was a member of this club at the Westwood, you say? So it would be easy for him to have had access?"

"Oh yes. Mind you," I added, "to be fair, it wouldn't be difficult for almost anyone to get in there. The pool and all the other facilities are open to hotel guests as well, and it's all very relaxed. No one actually asks to see your membership card."

"Right. Well, thank you, Sheila. I'd better get on to that. I suppose that blow on the head *might* have been enough to finish her off. She was certainly unconscious, so perhaps the murderer thought he'd succeeded. And again, in the steam room, from what you've told me, she very nearly died. They do sound like serious attempts on her life." Roger was silent for a moment, obviously readjusting his thoughts. Then he said briskly, "I think the rain's slackening off, I'd better jog back home."

"Oh, you don't want to do that!" I exclaimed. "I'll drive you back, and I promise to drop you off at the end of the road so that Jilly will never know!"

Chapter Thirteen

"They're having a committee meeting at Brunswick Lodge," Rosemary said, "to see who they can get to replace Freda. Apparently it's got to be at lunchtime to fit everyone in, and Jack's lumbered me with doing the refreshments. I don't suppose," she added, "you'd be an angel and give me a hand? It's just cutting sandwiches and putting out cheese and biscuits, really. I'll make a quiche and some sausage rolls at home today."

"Tomorrow?" I said. "Yes, I can manage that. What sort of time?"

"Well, the meeting's at one, so if we're there about eleven-thirty that should be all right. Bless you! Freda always used to see to that side of things, of course . . ."

When I got to Brunswick Lodge Rosemary was already there, cutting the crusts off a sliced loaf.

"Goodness!" I exclaimed. "You're using scissors. What a brilliant idea—so much less crumbly than fiddling about with a bread knife."

"I know, isn't it splendid? I copied it from Jilly. I must say the young do have some marvellous labour-saving ideas. She uses scissors for cutting up pizzas, too—much the easiest way!"

I unwrapped a slab of cheese and began to cut it up into portions and lay them out on a dish.

"The kettle has boiled," Rosemary said. "How about a cup of coffee?"

"I wonder who they'll get to be the new Chairman?"

"Who would be fool enough? It really is a thankless task."

"I suppose Sybil might be persuaded," I said. "There, is that coffee milky enough for you? She was always complaining about the way Freda ran things, perhaps she'd like to have a go herself. She might be quite good, really, she's nearly as bossy!"

"Yes, I suppose so." Rosemary paused in her task of buttering the bread. "This place still feels strange without Freda. I can't really believe that she's dead."

"I saw Roger on Sunday," I said. "I don't think they've got very far with the investigations and they don't seem to have found the weapon. It seems pretty certain it was the awl from the display—the wound was the right shape, apparently—but there's no sign of it."

"No," Rosemary agreed. "They certainly gave this place a good going over. Several times, actually. Very thorough. They looked everywhere. Lionel said that Sergeant Pope even wanted him to open up that old cupboard under the back stairs and Lionel said he couldn't because the key had been lost for ages. He got really huffy about it. You know what Lionel's like."

"Oh yes, I remember. Matthew Paisley thought he'd found a key in an old box, didn't he, but I don't quite know what happened about that, and anyway he died soon after, didn't he?"

"Lionel was being very officious about the whole thing, fussing around. I hope they don't make *him* Chairman!"

"No chance!" I laughed. "Everyone dislikes him too much!"

"No, it really ought to be Sybil. Oh, by the way, did I tell you that she and Pauline have joined the Westwood Club? Pauline thinks swimming might help her arthritis and, of course, if Pauline does something Sybil has to do the same."

"Yes, well, it might do Pauline some good. Several of the old dears who go there seem to think it does. There now, that's the cheese and biscuits sorted. Shall I cut up the quiche? Apparently Roger hadn't heard about Freda's nasty turn at the Westwood. He was quite interested when I told him. And, you know, really it does look pretty sinister if you think about it, far more than a coincidence. First, she got hit over the head, then she nearly died in the steam room, and then—well, then whoever it was finally finished her off."

"Mmm," Rosemary said. "It does sound peculiar when you put it like that." She looked up, frowning. "But honestly, who do you think could have murdered her? I mean—murder!"

"Laurence," I suggested. "He probably thought he was going to inherit something." I skirted round the truth because I didn't feel I could tell even Rosemary what Michael had told me about Freda and the will. "And perhaps his friend Jimmy was getting difficult about the amount of time Laurence had been spending with Freda."

"Oh, Jimmy!" Rosemary was instantly diverted. "Have you *seen* him? Jack and I ran into them in the bank the other day. I thought he was tremendous fun, but Jack, as you can imagine, was *not* impressed!"

"I had lunch with them in the Old Ship the other day," I said. "Well, I more or less *forced* Laurence to invite me to join them. He wasn't a bit keen. I got the distinct impression that the last thing he wanted was for Jimmy to come racing down to

Taviscombe to see if there were any pickings from Freda's will!"

"Do you really think Laurence could have killed her?"

"Well, he was the one who found her here when she was hit on the head, and he was the one who persuaded her to join the Westwood. I mean, he must have known about the steam room. And I don't think he's got an alibi for the time she was actually murdered. He's a pretty self-centred sort of person and I should think he'd be fairly ruthless if he was going after something he wanted. After all, he did make a dead set at Freda and I can't believe it was just for the theatres and the clothes and so forth." I got out the knives and forks and laid them on a tray. "Oh, I don't know. He *could* have done it. But perhaps I want him to be the murderer because I like him less than anyone else we know. And," I began to fold the paper napkins in half and put them on the plates, "it does *have* to be someone we know, someone Freda knew, doesn't it?"

Rosemary sighed. "Yes, I suppose it does. But *who*? Who'd have a motive?"

"I thought about Emily," I said. "She has a motive, all right, but there's no way she could have known where Freda would be at any particular time. And if you think about the other attempts (if that's what they were), then it simply couldn't have been her. And no, I can't think of anyone else . . ."

"Oh well," Rosemary said, briskly wrapping cling-film over the plates of sandwiches, "we'd better leave it to Roger to sort out. After all, it is his job."

"True," I agreed, "but it does sort of nag away at one."

We took the food and plates into the committee room and laid them all out in readiness.

"There we are, then," Rosemary said. "Now if we leave the coffee and the cups and things ready, they can jolly well make their own."

"By the way," I said as we were leaving, "I'm going to have tea with your mother tomorrow. I haven't been to see her for ages and I really feel very guilty."

"Yes, she told me you were going. I'm so glad, Sheila. She's an old devil sometimes, but she's been a bit low the last few weeks and I'm sure it will do her good to see you."

I've always had to brace myself to pay a visit to Mrs. Dudley. It's something I've felt all my life, ever since, as an awkward schoolgirl, she undermined my precarious self-confidence with some sharp glance or critical remark. But Rosemary has always been my best friend (ever since our first weeks at school) and facing her mother is the price I've had to pay.

Elsie, her faithful slave, drew me to one side as she opened the door. "I'm so pleased you've come, Mrs. Malory," she whispered. "She's not been herself at all lately. Seeing you will brighten her up."

Mrs. Dudley was sitting beside the fire. She is one of the few people I know who still have a coal fire ("I cannot stand those stupid electric things—they give out no sort of heat!"). Although she was bolt upright in her chair, she seemed to have shrunk since I saw her last and looked very frail. She was, as always, impeccably dressed in an expensive jersey wool suit from Estelle's and her hair was freshly set. It was a dull winter's afternoon and the lights hadn't been turned on. The firelight glittered on the diamond brooch she wore on her lapel and on the rings on her fingers, now swollen with arthritis. I was touched to see that her nails had been done with her usual pale pink varnish. It suddenly occurred to me what an effort it must be for her nowadays simply to get herself up and dressed each morning, let alone maintain her own rigorous standards of appearance, and I mentally saluted her gallantry.

She gave a slight start as I entered the room, as if her thoughts had been far away, but she gave me her old sharp glance and once again I was a young girl, conscious of a crooked seam in my stocking and a cardigan with a button hanging loose.

I gave her the peck on the cheek that was part of our ritual and put on the table by her side the pot of hyacinths I had brought.

"They're beautiful, Sheila," she said, "and how kind of you to remember that I like the white ones best." She leaned forward to smell the flowers and then picked up the pot and handed it back to me. "Just put them on that tray, will you, that pot will mark the table if we leave them here."

Duly chastened, I put the hyacinths on the tray she indicated and sat down as Elsie brought in the tea trolley, ladened as it always had been with sandwiches, scones, and a variety of cakes, and I thought again of the effort that had been made (mostly by Elsie, it is true, but still the ordering and the supervising had been hers) to keep things as they had always been.

Once again I nervously wielded the heavy silver teapot and remembered to rinse out the delicate bone china cups with warm water from the silver water jug before pouring the tea into them. This performance successfully completed and with one of Elsie's exquisite scones on my plate, I was able to relax slightly and answer Mrs. Dudley's questions about the doings of those members of Taviscombe society that she deemed worthy of her interest. It seemed to me, though, that although the inquisition was as thorough as usual, Mrs. Dudley was not giving it her customary attention. Her voice was quiet and almost listless and I thought that perhaps the exertion of all the preparations had tired her.

She did not eat as much as usual, merely asking me to cut her a small slice of Elsie's Victoria sponge, which she crumbled and picked at, and I felt sad to think that even the indomitable Mrs. Dudley was growing old and, one day in the not too distant future, would no longer be with us. The room was very hot and the scent of the hyacinths, usually so fresh and spring-like, suddenly seemed sickly and oppressive. A coal, burning through, fell into the hearth and I knelt down, feeling the heat of the fire on my face, and, taking the tongs and the little brass shovel from their stand in the hearth, put it back again.

For a moment we were both silent, then, for want of anything else to say I observed, "I saw Pam Nelson the other day, at the school reunion. Do you remember her?"

"Pamela Nelson? Pamela Nelson? Yes, I most certainly do remember her." The voice, miraculously, was strong again and she seemed to snap back to attention. "Her father kept that newsagent's shop in the Avenue. It was a very good business before the war, that was before Smith's came, and he was a town councillor for several years. Her mother was a schoolteacher before she married him—elementary school, of course—but quite a well-educated person. She was secretary of the Taviscombe W.I. one of the years when I was president. There was a boy as well as Pamela, but he was killed in the war."

"Yes," I said, "I remember."

"Pamela," Mrs. Dudley continued, "was very wild as a girl. She had quite a reputation. I was very sorry for her parents, who were respectable people. He was one of the churchwardens at St. Andrews."

"Wild?" I queried.

Mrs. Dudley pursed her lips in her old familiar way. "Young men," she said. "Oh, I don't suppose people would think anything of it nowadays, more's the pity! But before the war a young woman's reputation was important."

"Young men?"

"There was the Ditchley boy—his father soon put a stop to that! And then John Blackford and his brother Kenneth as well, I believe."

I marvelled at Mrs. Dudley's unfailing ability to pull these names, long forgotten by me, fresh from her memory.

"Then, of course, there was Richard Lewis."

"Ah yes, Richard," I said. "I gather that was quite serious."

Mrs. Dudley leaned forward slightly in her chair. "I certainly believe they would have been engaged—and the way they were carrying on, they certainly *should* have been engaged—but his mother was a widow, you know, with very little money, and he had his way to make in the world and he couldn't afford to take on extra responsibilities. And then the war came."

"Richard joined up early on?"

"Oh yes, the Air Force. I believe he had been in some sort of Reserve or whatever they called it, so he went straight away."

"And Pam?"

"She went to London to some hospital or other," Mrs. Dudley said. "She certainly didn't come back home for several years. I think there was something very odd going on there because her parents never mentioned her and, if I chanced to enquire, they were really quite brusque."

I could imagine Mrs. Dudley's "enquiries," and was not surprised that she had been met with an evasive response.

"And Richard?" I asked.

"He came to see his mother when he had leave, that was while he was still in England."

"He must have been a very glamorous figure," I said.

"The young women certainly threw themselves at his head," Mrs. Dudley said disapprovingly. "But after Pamela went away like that, he only had eyes for Freda Clark. She was a striking girl, much handsomer than Pamela Nelson, but even then there was something disagreeable about her. And now she's got herself killed."

She made it sound as if it was somehow Freda's fault—and, I suppose, in a way it was.

"Poor Richard," I said.

"That woman completely ruined his life," Mrs. Dudley said vehemently. "Leading him on like that and then marrying someone else." She finished off the piece of Victoria sponge on her plate. "I think," she said, "I might manage a piece of walnut cake, if you would be so kind as to cut one for me."

"And Richard never saw Pam again?" I asked, cutting a substantial slice."After he joined up, I mean."

"Not in Taviscombe," said Mrs. Dudley. "What may have happened in *London,* I do not know." Mrs. Dudley disapproved of London as being out of her jurisdiction. "I believe she did very well for herself in the end."

"Yes," I said. "Her husband's a very distinguished paediatrician."

Mrs. Dudley gave a slight sniff. Her opinion of doctors, however eminent, is not high.

"She was looking very glamorous at the reunion," I said provocatively. "Her hair's blonde now."

"Quite ridiculous in a woman of her age! But then," she said with some satisfaction, "breeding, or the lack of it, will out."

The walnut cake, I saw, had gone and Mrs. Dudley now reached forward for a piece of shortbread.

When I rose to go, after several other reputations had been torn to shreds, I was delighted to see that, temporarily at least, Mrs. Dudley was her old self again. On an impulse I bent and gave her a swift hug.

She looked up in surprise, and gave me one of her rare smiles. "Don't leave it so long before you come again," she said. "It does me good to see old friends."

Elsie, who had come into the room to see me out, switched on the lights and Mrs. Dudley looked at me, one of her old, sharp looks. "Good heavens, Sheila," she said, "what on *earth* have you done to your hair?"

Chapter Fourteen

Talking to Mrs. Dudley about Pam Nelson made me think of Richard, and when I got home I tried to ring again and eventually, when I rang the operator, she said that the phone seemed to have been left off the hook and there was nothing she could do.

"It really is a bit worrying," I said to Michael that evening. "I haven't seen him since the day Freda died. Rosemary says that no one seems to have seen him around. I think I'd better try and call tomorrow."

But though, next morning, I rang the bell several times, there was no reply and nothing to show if he was there or not. At least there was no accumulation of milk and newspapers that might give some reason for alarm—simply nothing.

I went on into the town to do some shopping and, as I was crossing the Avenue, to my great surprise, I saw Pam Nelson going into Boots. I hurried in after her and touched her lightly on the arm.

"Hello, Pam," I said. "I thought you'd gone back to London ages ago."

She turned quickly in surprise. "Oh, Sheila! Yes, I'm still here. Hugh had to get back, but when I went to see Uncle Leslie at West Lodge I found he was quite bright, perfectly compos mentis, and *so* pleased to see me, so I thought I'd stay on for a bit to be with him."

"That's nice," I said. "Where are you staying?"

"Oh, I'm at the Esplanade. Isn't it funny, when I was very young I thought it was frightfully grand. I used to watch people in evening dress going in to the dinner dances they had before the war. It seemed so glamorous! And now—well, it's just a rather ordinary, not very special seaside hotel."

"I know," I agreed. "They had the Hunt Ball there sometimes. I remember going to one when I was about sixteen and I felt like something in a Hollywood film. Actually, it's a bit like that old French film, what was it called? *Un Carnet de Bal,* I think it was. All about how the things we remember about our youth weren't really like that at all."

"It sounds a bit metaphysical," Pam laughed, "but I know what you mean. Especially at school reunions."

"Oh, I know! It's odd. People still mostly look

like they did when they were young, but sort of *blurred.* What did Shakespeare say about devouring time blunting the lion's paws? I always think of that when I see those old statues with bits worn away!"

Pam laughed again, though in an abstracted sort of way. "Sheila," she said, in quite a different tone of voice, "are you doing anything this morning?"

I looked at her in surprise. "No," I said, "at least nothing important. Why?"

She was silent for a moment and then, as if changing her mind about what she had been going to say, she said, "Oh, I just had a fancy to drive out to see Snowdrop Valley again. It's still the same, I hope?"

Snowdrop Valley is a local beauty spot, which in mid-February is famous for its carpet of snowdrops.

"Yes. It's more or less as it used to be, though since it's been on television a couple of times a lot more people go there. Still, because you have to leave your car and walk part of the way, it's fairly unspoilt."

"Do you feel like coming with me?" Pam asked. "It would be nice to have company."

"Yes, I'd love to. Let's take my car. It's just across the road. It'll save going back to the hotel for yours."

"Fine," she said. "I probably wouldn't remember the way, anyhow, after all this time."

As we drove along the Exe Valley we talked of ordinary things—the changes Pam had seen in Taviscombe, what articles I was writing, how Michael was getting on—none of the things I wanted to talk to her about and not, I felt, what she had originally intended to say to me. I stopped the car in the layby just before the road to the valley and we got out. In her belted camel-hair coat and with a scarf tied over the blonde hair, Pam looked much more as I remembered her.

"I had to buy a pair of sensible shoes," she said, holding out a foot for me to see. "I'd forgotten how *muddy* everywhere is down here in winter!"

"I know," I agreed, "I seem to live in boots or sandals, nothing in between."

We walked slowly down the lane that runs along the floor of the valley. There were snowdrops everywhere, massed on the banks and on the grassy verges and, beyond, the fields were white with them, while in the woods behind the fields there were great patches of white, like snow lying thick among the trees.

Pam stopped and looked about her. "It's fantastic, isn't it?" she said. "So beautiful! So peaceful! I can hardly believe that there are still places like this left in the world."

"It's nice to have it to ourselves. It's always better to come in the morning," I said prosaically. "More people come in the afternoon for a little run in the car. Shall we go across this field and into the wood? I particularly love to see the way they grow all the way along the stream there."

We picked our way carefully across the field—though the snowdrops were growing so thickly that it was difficult not to tread on them—and into the wood. Here, the distant noise of the traffic on the road above was drowned by the rushing water swirling past, almost right up to the top of the bank, the white foam, where it ran over rocks or fell over little waterfalls, less white than the flowers around it.

"The water's high," I said. "We've had so much rain lately."

"Sheila." Pam stood quite still. "I want to talk to you."

"Of course," I said. "Look, it's not too cold. Shall we sit on this log?"

"I don't really know how to begin," Pam said.

"Is it about Richard?" I asked.

"Yes. Yes, it is."

"I've been so worried about him. I've tried to ring several times, after—you know—after Freda died, but he's not answering the phone and there's no reply when I've called. Have you seen him?"

"Yes. I've seen him," she said slowly, "and I'm worried about him too."

We were both silent for a moment. In the cold, cruel winter light she looked old and tired, her face criss-crossed by lines under her careful make-up.

"Did something happen at the reunion dinner?" I asked.

She nodded, as if she couldn't bring herself to actually speak.

"And earlier, at the school," I persisted. "You and Freda in the cloisters."

She gave me a slight smile. "You're very observant," she said.

"Richard looked so terrible," I said, "and afterwards, when I saw him leaning on the sea wall—I've never seen anyone look like that!"

"He'd had a shock," Pam said carefully. "And so had I."

"Can you tell me?" I asked. "Would it help?"

"I think I have to tell you. I must go away soon, back to London, and I need to explain to someone about Richard. I need someone to look out for him, and I know you're fond of him . . ."

"Yes, of course. But as I said, he doesn't reply."

"I will tell him that I have told you everything," she said. "He will need someone when I have gone."

"Is it to do with Freda?" I asked.

She nodded. "Yes, it was always Freda." She took off her gloves and laid them, folded neatly, on her lap. "From the very beginning we were rivals, in competition, whether it was who was to be top in History at school, who had the latest fashion, who had the most enviable boyfriend. I had Richard. He was *so* good looking in those days! And such fun. Lively and intelligent, so full of life!" She looked at me quizzically. "I expect you find that hard to believe now?"

"Not really," I said. "I can remember him in the 1950s. All my friends thought he was very glamorous—brave fighter pilot and all that."

"Yes," she said, "Richard had a good war. He was very brave or, at least, he was very reckless."

She was silent for a moment. "And Freda?" I prompted her. "I gather Freda was jealous of you and Richard."

"Oh yes. She was much prettier than I was, and she could have had practically any boy she wanted, but, of course, she wanted Richard." She gave a little laugh. "She was always making up to him, flattering him, but Richard was in love with me, bless him, and simply didn't notice it! I tried to tell him what she was up to, but he didn't believe me. She pretended to be my friend, you see, and Richard—dear, simple, honest Richard—believed her and thought I was being unfair to her."

"Oh, Freda could be very convincing when she wanted," I said.

"It was in the winter of 1939," Pam went on, "when everything was so muddled and uncertain. There was the feeling that we were living on the edge of something. It was still the phony war, the reality hadn't really sunk in yet. But there were things—those newsreels of refugees, with their belongings piled on carts, trudging along roads that led to God knows where. . . . We suddenly knew then what war was like, for ordinary people, I mean."

She gave a little shiver and pulled her coat closer round her. "Richard was in the RAF Volunteer Reserve, so he'd been among the first to go, and I'd decided that I was going to London to be a nurse—I was desperate to be in the thick of things—and I'd been accepted at St. Mary's. It was very strange in Taviscombe at that time. There were a lot of children and teenagers, evacuees mostly, but apart from the farm workers, nearly all the young people, people of my age, had gone. A few weeks before I left for London, Richard had some leave and came back to Taviscombe to see his mother. And to see me. It was such a strange time. Idyllic in some ways, agonisingly sad in others. We were very much in love and didn't know when we'd see each other again. Well, you've seen the movies, you can imagine how it was. We only had a week, then Richard went away to his training camp and a little while after that I went up to London.

"It was all very new and exciting. I won't say it took my mind off missing Richard, but I was so busy, so exhausted at the end of every day, that it helped. We wrote to each other, of course, but then I had a note from him to say that he was being moved and not to write until he sent me his new address."

I was beginning to feel very cold, sitting there, but I didn't want to interrupt Pam's story. I thrust my hands deep into my pockets and waited for her to continue.

"It was just about then," Pam said, "that I discovered that I was pregnant." She gave me a wry smile. "Well, you know what it was like in those days, shameful, disgrace on the family, all that. My father was a churchwarden and very conscious of his position in the town. I don't say that he'd have disowned me, but it would have broken his heart. It seemed to me that there was only one thing to be done—Richard and I had to get married. It was logical, after all. We'd always planned to, when the war was over and Richard had started to make his way in the world. I wanted—I needed so much to write to him, to tell him what had happened. It was infuriating not to be in touch.

"Then I thought I'd go and see his mother. Not to tell her about the baby, of course, she'd have been so shocked, but to see if she'd had any news of Richard. I knew I wouldn't be able to get any time off from the hospital, so one morning, after I came off night duty, I caught the early train from Paddington and came down to Taviscombe. There was a direct line in those days, so I knew I could do it there and back in a day, in time to be back on night duty.

"I went round to her house—she lived in one of those cottages on the quay—but there was no reply and her next door neighbour told me she'd gone away to stay with her sister in Bristol."

Pam was leaning forward now, almost oblivious of my presence, as she relived that day. "I was pretty miserable, as you can imagine. The disappointment of Mrs. Lewis being away and then being tired after my night duty, not to mention feeling pretty groggy, as you often are in the early months of pregnancy. I walked across the road and sat down in one of the shelters looking out to sea, trying to think what to do. I didn't really want to go and see my parents, because they'd ask questions I didn't want to answer, and there were several hours before I could get a train back to London. Although it was winter, one of the cafés in the Avenue was open and I went in there to get a cup of tea. To my surprise, who should come in but Freda.

"I suppose it was because I was in a weakened sort of state that I was really quite glad to see her, a familiar face, after all, and, having been away for a while, the old antagonism between us seemed to have faded. She was very friendly and nice and I thought perhaps she'd changed—lots of people had, somehow, because of the war.

"I told her that I wanted to get in touch with Richard and that his mother was away. She was very sympathetic and said that her mother knew Mrs. Lewis's sister's telephone number and she'd ring up and see if she had Richard's new address. I was so grateful and gave her my address at the nurses' home and went off to catch my train. A few days later I had a note from Freda with the address of Richard's camp, somewhere in Lincolnshire. Of course I wrote to him straight away and waited anxiously for his answer. But he didn't answer and so I wrote again, in case the letter had been lost in the post. But no reply, nothing. I couldn't believe it. I was desperate and tried to get a phone number to ring him, but, in the war, such things just weren't possible. I thought I'd go up to Lincolnshire and see him, but there was no way I could get leave from the hospital and I wasn't brave enough simply to go missing. I honestly didn't know what to do.

"Then I had a letter from my mother, who mentioned in passing that Richard had been in Taviscombe for a few days' leave the week before I had been there and that, as I probably knew, he was now on his way to Canada for training." She shook her head. "I simply couldn't believe it. There was no way that the Richard I knew would go off like that without a word, especially now he knew about the baby. But it seemed that I'd been wrong about him. I thought that perhaps even the best of men, faced with that situation, might panic and simply cut and run. I was very bitter and, as you can imagine, very worried. It seemed that there was only one thing left for me to do. It wasn't so very difficult in London, in the war, to find someone who'd get rid of a baby, even if it was illegal, if you paid them well enough. One of the girls in the nurses' home gave me an address and—well, that was that."

Her lip quivered for a moment, then she went on.

"I got through the war. The blitz came soon after that and life was too hectic and too harrowing to dwell too long on the past. Just keeping alive, living from day to day, seeing all the pain and distress around you. . . . Then after the war I stayed on at

St. Mary's. I met Hugh and we got married. It's been a good life. Except—well, except that the abortion wasn't properly done. I've never been able to have another child."

She buried her face in her hands and broke down, sobbing. I put my arm around her shoulders and sat there not knowing what to say. I focused my eyes on a clump of snowdrops at our feet, each flower with its green-veined, frilled petals perfect and unique and, all around, the hundreds of thousands of snowdrops, each subtly different, as people are different.

"I'm sorry." Pam raised her head. "Just telling you brought it all back."

"Let's go back to the car," I said, "it's getting very cold."

We retraced our steps in silence and got into the car.

"I'll put the heater on to warm us up," I said. I made no attempt to move off because I knew there was a lot more that Pam needed to tell me.

"About Richard," I said. "There was some mix-up, wasn't there? I simply can't believe that he could have abandoned you like that!"

Pam gave a bitter laugh. "Oh no," she said, "there was no mix-up. It was quite deliberate."

"I don't understand."

"Freda, of course, dear Freda. She gave me a

false address. No wonder the letter never reached him. By that time he was on his way to Canada for six months."

"But surely she knew you'd have been bound to find out! Richard would have written to you."

"She'd seen him when he was in Taviscombe, before I went down, and told him that I'd found someone else and wanted to break off with him."

"And he believed her?"

"Oh yes. She said that I couldn't bear to tell him myself and had asked her to break it to him. He thought she was my friend, you see, so he believed her. And, of course, she laid it on very thick, how upset I was and how these things happened in wartime. You know the sort of thing."

"It's unbelievable!"

"It was a bit of luck for her, running into me like that in Taviscombe. I suppose she was going to write to me, telling me the same story about Richard finding someone else and so on."

"And neither of you found out?"

"No. I didn't come back to Taviscombe—except very briefly to see my family when Jack died—and then, after the war, Hugh and I were abroad quite a bit. Richard, of course, was in Canada and then in Kent with Fighter Command. That's when he got his DFC. I gather he did some rather reckless things because he didn't greatly care if he lived or died. Freda kept in touch—she was in the Wrens by then—and made him think she cared for him so he came to depend on her. But then she met this rich man and married him, leaving Richard high and dry. Still, by then he was hooked, she'd got him completely under her spell."

"Yes," I said sadly, "right to the bitter end."

"Not quite to the end," Pam said.

"No, of course! The reunion! You found out what had happened?"

"I'd had a sort of suspicion for some time," she said. "Just a niggle. The address she gave me. One of Hugh's friends was in Fighter Command and when I mentioned this base in Lincolnshire he looked puzzled and said he'd never heard of one there. That's where the Bomber Command stations were. Then, just after the war, I heard from my mother about how Freda and Richard were always together and I began to wonder. By then, though, I had Hugh and our life together, we lived far away from Taviscombe and I didn't really want to open old wounds."

"But you came back for the reunion."

Pam gave a little laugh. "Well, you know how it is. Curiosity, I suppose. You want to see how your contemporaries have worn. So I put on my glad rags and came down."

"You did cause something of a sensation." I laughed.

"Good. I meant to. But, oh, I was so shocked to see how Richard had changed. A dried-up old man! I think that's what made me tackle Freda about what I suspected she'd done."

"Is that what you were both arguing about when Rosemary and I saw you in the cloisters?" I asked.

"Yes. She was appalled to see me at the reunion, of course, and at first when I faced her with what I was sure she'd done she denied it. But then I said I'd ask Richard." Pam smiled. "She admitted it then, and tried to laugh it off. Can you believe that? It was all a long time ago, we were all very young, and anyway, things had worked out well for me, hadn't they?"

"No!"

"Oh yes. That's what she said. I don't know how I didn't hit her!"

"I can imagine! What did you say?"

"I didn't. I simply walked away and left her."

There was a pause.

"And then you told Richard?" I asked. "At the reunion dinner? I saw you go off together into the conservatory and then—and then Richard came back looking like death."

"It was the baby, of course. I think he could have coped with the rest, but not the baby."

"His whole life," I said slowly, "would have been different. A normal happy life with a wife and children, instead of that sterile, miserable existence, hanging around after Freda—Freda, who'd been the reason he missed out on *everything*! Oh, poor, poor Richard. It must have been insupportable!"

"Yes." Pam put her hand on mine. "Thank you for caring about him, Sheila. You can understand he needs all his friends, all the help he can get."

"Yes, of course," I said, "anything I can do. If only he'll let me." I looked at her. "And you, Pam, what it must have done to you!"

She shrugged. "It was a bad moment, but different for me. I'd suspected something, it wasn't such a shock. And then, I have Hugh and we've had a wonderful life together, even if . . . well, there it is." She was silent for a moment and then she said, "So you see how it seemed right to both of us that Freda should die."

Chapter Fifteen

For a moment I stared at her, unable to take in her meaning, and then, when I had, unable to believe what I had heard. Pam, watching my face, smiled slightly.

"No," she said, "I didn't murder her. Though, God knows, I felt enough hatred for her." I started to speak, but she went on. "Honestly I didn't. Actually, I have an alibi."

"No, really . . ."

"When Freda was breathing her last I was at West Lodge with Uncle Leslie. I saw the Matron when I arrived and again as I was leaving, she will remember. And I saw Maureen Philips—we had quite a little chat—and Olive, Freda's cousin, as well."

"No, really," I repeated, "I'm sure you didn't kill Freda."

Pam looked at me enquiringly. "Would you have been so sure if I hadn't had an alibi?"

I nodded. "Yes, I would," I said immediately. "You're not the sort of person who'd let an injury, however dreadful, destroy the rest of your life. You're too . . ." I searched fruitlessly for the appropriate word and finished lamely, "too *practical*, I suppose."

Pam laughed outright. "Well, there's a recommendation!"

"No," I said, "you know what I mean. You wouldn't let anything from the past eat away at you and poison the present, and you wouldn't let one act of revenge jeopardise your future. You'd do—well, what you have done. Put things behind you and get on with the rest of your life."

"Yes," Pam said slowly, "I suppose that's what I have done."

"There's a lot to be said for it," I said. "When Peter died quite young—the same month as my mother, actually, I almost gave up. Of course, I had to be strong for Michael's sake, but I did make a conscious decision not to keep looking back. It was the only way for me."

"Yes," Pam said, "we're quite alike in a lot of ways."

"That's why I am quite sure you didn't kill Freda."

I was silent for a moment and then I said tentatively, "I'm sure about you. But what about Richard?"

Pam shook her head. "That's just it," she said. "I don't know, I really don't know."

I sighed. "Oh dear, how difficult this is."

"He had the motive," Pam said. "He certainly had the motive. Sheila, you've known him for a long time, all those years when I haven't seen him, all those years, when he's changed so much from the Richard I used to know. Do you think he might have killed Freda?"

I rubbed my cold fingers together to try to generate a little warmth. "Yes," I said eventually. "Yes, I think after what you told him, he'd be quite capable of killing her."

"Oh God." Pam closed her eyes for a moment. "You're right, of course. I just didn't want to admit it, even to myself."

"I shall never forget his face that night," I said.

"No. Since then he's been acting very strangely. Like a zombie, almost. I went to see him the next morning, but I couldn't really get him to talk to me."

"I called round," I said, "but he didn't answer the door, and I tried to ring but he's left the phone off the hook."

"I don't think he can face anyone yet," Pam

said. "I had to call through the letter box to say who it was before he let me in."

I put the car into gear. "Come on," I said. "We're both frozen. Let's go to the pub at Wheddon Cross and get a good strong drink and some lunch."

"Good idea!" She paused in the act of fastening her seat belt. "Oh God! That *bloody* woman! Even now she's dead she's still wrecking people's lives."

That evening, with Foss on my lap and the dogs sleeping heavily on my feet, I told Michael Pam's story.

"Well, it certainly doesn't look as if she did it," he said. "She seems to have a pretty solid alibi—all those people. Anyway, she wasn't here when the other things happened."

He paused for a moment and then went on, "So if Emily wasn't here, nor Pam Nelson, that leaves Richard or Laurence Marvell."

"Or someone we haven't thought of."

"Well, yes. But those two both have a good motive. Hang on, though," Michael said, "Richard didn't know about Freda's deception of Pam until the reunion, so that slightly dishes his motive. For the first two attacks, anyway."

"Not really," I said. "It just gives him a different one."

"How do you mean?"

"Well, he was already at the end of his tether with Freda. He'd proposed yet again, remember, and had been turned down. So cruelly, in fact, that he wished she was dead."

"That's true. Come to think of it, the first two attempts were a bit half-hearted. It was only the last one that was, well, *thorough*, you might say, as if whoever it was was determined to finish her off this time."

"That certainly does seem to fit Richard," I said. "But then, really, is Richard capable of *murder*? He's always been so gentle. Could he really bring himself to kill anybody?"

"But he has," Michael said.

"What?"

"In the war. Fighter pilots killed other fighter pilots."

"Yes, but . . ."

"And even if it's just pressing a button to fire a machine gun, you have to be aware that you're actually aiming that machine gun at another human being with the intention of killing them."

"But that was a case of self-preservation," I protested. "If he hadn't killed those enemy airmen he'd have been killed himself."

"And if he hadn't killed Freda he would have been totally destroyed himself."

"But that's different!"

"Not really. Not when you're in the sort of state that Richard was in. People do very strange things under that sort of pressure."

"I suppose they do."

Over the last couple of years it has been borne in upon me that although Michael is so many years younger than I am, his time as a solicitor has brought him into contact with situations and emotions—usually of a dark and complex kind—that I have no experience of. Tessa made a little grunting noise in her sleep and Tris raised his head for a moment to look at her, then also subsided into sleep.

"Getting into Brunswick Lodge both times would have been easy for Richard," Michael said thoughtfully, "and he knows his way about in there. I mean, he'd know where Freda would have been. But what about the swimming club at the Westwood? He wasn't a member, was he?"

"That wouldn't have been a problem. You're supposed to sign in at the reception desk, but half the time the girls there are coming and going and don't take any notice. It would be easy to slip past. Anyway, the pool's open to hotel residents as well as members, so no one would have questioned him. He could have changed into swimming trunks and goggles and hung about in the men's changing room waiting his chance."

"Wouldn't there have been other people there?" Michael asked.

"Not really," I replied. "It's usually quite empty around that time, which is why Freda used to go then."

"Right. So he waits till she's in the steam room and jams the door and turns up the heat. . . ."

"Yes," I interrupted, "and then simply turns round that Pool Open/Pool Closed notice to keep other members out."

"Did anyone say anything about the notice when they found her?" Michael asked.

"I don't think so. No, wait a minute. When I got there—just after they'd taken Freda away—I saw Denise, one of the hotel staff, turning it round to say Pool Closed. So perhaps Richard (if it was Richard) hung about and turned it round to say Open after the pool attendant found Freda, so that nobody would know that something peculiar was going on."

"Would that be possible?"

"Oh yes, there are a couple of hotel lounges near the entrance to the pool with lots of alcoves with large armchairs where you could hide away quite easily, especially in the afternoon when there's only a skeleton staff on duty."

"How would Richard have known, though, that she was going to be in the steam room then?"

"Oh, you know what Freda's like, always telling anyone who'll listen about her every movement. It would be just like her to have been boasting at Brunswick Lodge about what she was going to do in the gym and using the steam room and so forth, so that people would think how active and youthful she was."

"So Richard could have done it."

"Yes, he could. But so could Laurence Marvell," I said.

"I thought he was in Taunton."

"Buying embroidery silks. Yes, well, he could easily have got them at some other time. It's not much of an alibi. And, when Freda was attacked that first time, Laurence was the one who found her, so we know he was around."

"Where was Richard that day?" Michael asked.

"I don't know. In fact we don't know where he was at any of the times, do we?"

"True."

"And when Freda was murdered he says he went for a walk. Which, of course, might well be exactly what he *would* do after all those awful revelations the night before. I wonder if anyone saw him? Goodness, all this is very confusing."

"You'll have to have a chat with Roger and see who's got an alibi for what," Michael said.

"Laurence Marvell says he was driving down from London at the time when Freda was killed," I said. "*That's* going to be difficult to prove."

But, as it happened, it wasn't.

The next morning Roger telephoned. "I thought you'd like to know," he said. "Laurence Marvell *has* got an alibi."

"Really? But how . . . ?"

"He told me he stopped off at the service station at Leigh Delamere, so I got North Somerset CID to show his photo to the girls who were on the cash desks there that evening and one of them recognised him."

"Good heavens!"

"Apparently she had to give him change for a twenty-pound note for one cup of coffee. And, anyway, she said she remembered him because she thought he looked ever so like Mel Gibson!"

"Really? Yes, perhaps he does in a blurred sort of way."

"So that's Laurence Marvell accounted for."

"Yes, I suppose it is."

"You sound disappointed."

"Well, he was such a good suspect—you know, the money and all that. And, to be honest, I never really liked him."

"I agree," Roger said sardonically, "that it would be very convenient if all villains were unlikable. Oh well, back to square one."

"Which is?"

"To be honest, I'm damned if I know. The daughter and this man Marvell, the two people with the obvious motive—money—are both out of the picture. Do you have any ideas?"

"Ideas?" I echoed.

"Motive? Means? Opportunity? Can you think of anyone else who wanted her dead?"

I must have paused for rather too long, because Roger said sharply, "Sheila, *do* you know of anyone?"

"Well, yes," I said, "I do know someone with a motive, but she couldn't have done it because she's got an alibi, and anyway, I'm really sure she didn't do it."

"I think you'd better tell me about her."

"Actually, she only told me about it yesterday," I said placatingly. "She's Pam Nelson—or rather Pam Watson, that's her married name, it's just that I still *think* of her as Pam Nelson. She used to know Freda in the old days, they were at school together. Well, it seems that years ago Freda did something dreadful that affected Pam's life and Pam only found out about it recently, at the school reunion. Pam did have a motive, she admitted it quite freely, but when Freda was killed Pam was at West Lodge visiting her uncle and lots of people saw her there."

"I see. Well, I must have a word with Pam Watson. Where is she to be found?"

"She was staying at the Esplanade," I said, slightly flustered at the thought of Roger interviewing Pam and thinking what might come out about Richard, "but she may have gone back to London by now. But really, Roger, do you *need* to see her? It would be very upsetting for her to go through it all again. Couldn't you just check with the Matron at West Lodge? Surely that would be enough?"

"Why do I get the feeling that you're not telling me everything you know?" Roger said. "Come along, now, Sheila, you know as well as I do all that stuff about withholding information?"

"Yes, of course I do. It's just—well, it's not that easy. Pam told me all this in confidence . . ."

"And does any of it have a bearing on Freda Spencer's murder?"

"I honestly don't know. There's nothing *concrete,* no proof or evidence or anything, just an idea, a feeling. Please don't press me about it,

Roger. Perhaps you *had* better talk to Pam. If she tells you, then I won't feel I've betrayed a friend."

"Poor Sheila. I'm sorry if I put you in an invidious position. But, after all, murder is murder, and not something to be taken lightly."

"Yes, I do see that. I'm sorry, it's the old heart and head thing, isn't it? Anyway, have a word with Pam, you'll be able to make your own judgment then."

After he rang off I telephoned the Esplanade to warn Pam. "I'm frightfully sorry," I said. "I'm afraid he sort of bounced me into it. It's a bit awkward with him being my god-daughter's husband. But I didn't go into any sort of detail. I just said that Freda had done something awful, but I didn't say what, or mention Richard or anything. And I did tell him you'd got an alibi . . ."

"Oh well, it can't be helped," Pam said. "I do see it must have been difficult for you. The thing is to keep Richard's name out of it."

"Can you do that?"

"I'll try. I'll be vague and just say 'my boyfriend' and try and make it seem that it was someone who doesn't live in Taviscombe any more."

"That would be fine," I said, relieved. "But Pam, what about Richard? What should we do?"

"I have to go back to London the day after tomorrow. I'll go and see him and see what I can find out. I'll tell him you want to see him, too. I just hope I can get through to him this time."

"Yes, I hope you can. Let me know how you get on, Pam. Oh, and what you say to Roger, too. Poor Richard, even if he did kill Freda, I don't believe I could find it in my heart to blame him."

"I think," Pam said viciously, "that if he had killed Freda, there might well be a great many people who'd want to put up a statue to him!"

Chapter Sixteen

I always like to give the flowers at St. James's on the Sunday nearest to the anniversary of my mother's death, and I usually go along on the Saturday to arrange them. As I opened the heavy oak door and went in, the church felt cold and I saw that the vicar was fiddling with the thermostat at the back of the church near the font.

"Good morning, Vicar," I said. "Something wrong with the heating?"

He greeted me absently and then raised his head and said, "It's no good, I really don't know *what's* wrong. I shall have to get one of the church wardens to have a look at it before tomorrow. I'm so sorry, Mrs. Malory, do forgive me. It's just that anything in the least *mechanical* and I'm quite lost!"

"Oh, I know," I said, "I'm just the same."

"And you have brought those beautiful flowers!"

"My mother's anniversary . . ."

"Ah yes, Mrs. . . . er . . ."

"Prior."

"Of course, Mrs. Prior. So many people have told me what a delightful person she was and what splendid work she did in the parish. I greatly regret not having known her."

Mr. Whipple is a relatively new incumbent. He's rather a dim young man and his sermons are flat and uninspired, but he's reinstated the old prayer book and the Authorised Version, for which I'm deeply grateful, since now I can feel comfortable again in church.

Looking beyond Mr. Whipple and down the nave I saw a small figure in one of the pews near the front. It was Olive. She was sitting, leaning forward, her head bowed, one hand in front of her face, presumably in prayer.

I instinctively lowered my voice. "I'll just go and put these flowers in water. I'll go round the back way to the vestry so that I don't disturb Olive."

"Olive? Ah, Miss Clark. Actually, I don't think you would disturb her. She's in here most days, talking to God."

"Oh. Oh, I see."

"I think," Mr. Whipple leaned towards me confidentially, "she is missing her cousin and she finds this *communion* a comfort."

"Yes, I'm sure she must."

"A little odd, perhaps," Mr. Whipple smiled benevolently, "to an outsider, the muttering and so forth. But each of us has our own path to the Lord, don't you agree?"

"Yes, of course."

"And I have always been very firm that the church should be kept unlocked at all times for those who need its spiritual comfort."

"I'm sure you're right."

"Indeed, only the other day I had an elderly gentleman in great distress—you may know him, a Mr. Lewis—greatly distressed, as I say, but I had a few words with him and we prayed together for a while and I do believe that he went away in a happier state of mind."

Mr. Whipple's gaze returned to the thermostat and an expression of annoyance crossed his face. "It's no good," he said. "I'll have to go and find Jim Baker. Nice to have had this chat . . ."

Mr. Whipple's indiscreet information dismayed me. The fact that Richard, never a churchgoer, had felt the need to go in search of some sort of comfort at St. James's somehow brought home to me the depths of his despair. I wondered if Mr.

Whipple's easy assumption of a happy outcome had indeed been so. I sincerely wished it had, but somehow I doubted it.

I left the church and re-entered it by the vestry door. The little room leading out of the vestry had a sink and a selection of vases, all more or less, as is the way with church vases, the wrong shape or size for the flowers I had brought. Still, after a little snipping and tweaking I managed to get them arranged reasonably well. I picked up the largest vase and took it through into the church. I'd been quite a long time arranging the flowers and assumed that Olive would have gone, but she was still there and I could hear a sort of murmuring coming from the pew where she was still sitting. As I leaned forward to place the vase at the bottom of the pulpit steps, she looked up.

"Why, Sheila," she said, "how nice to see you. And what lovely flowers."

"Hello, Olive. Yes, they're in memory of mother. She died ten years ago on Thursday."

"Ten years! It hardly seems possible! Such a wonderful person, so loving and kind. I do miss her."

I was relieved to find that Olive seemed to be her old self; the vicar's remark about talking to God, had, presumably, been a sort of ecclesiastical jargon.

"How is dear Michael?" she asked with her usual loving smile.

"He's fine. Very busy but enjoying life, I'm glad to say."

"And you, my dear?"

"Oh, not too bad. It's a depressing time of the year, though. I shall be glad when the spring comes!"

"It will come, dear, it will come. The good Lord will not fail us." She came towards me and took my hand. "Trust in the Lord, dear, and he will tell you what to do."

I smiled nervously. "Yes, I'm sure He will," I said.

"I have put my life in His hands," Olive said, "and He has made everything right."

I disengaged my hand gently. "That's wonderful," I said. "I'm so glad for you. Do forgive me, I must just go and get the rest of the flowers." I hung about in the vestry for a while until I heard her leave and then took the other vases into the church and came away.

I was disconcerted and vaguely disquieted by Olive's outbreak of religious fervor, but decided that it was probably a consequence of the shock of Freda's death, something that must have hit her very hard. Yet another example, I thought, of

Freda's influence extending beyond the grave. Still, I hoped that Olive's more frequent visits to Emily and her family would give her a new interest in life. What really occupied my mind was the thought of Richard, and when I got back home I tried to ring Pam Nelson at her hotel, but she wasn't there.

I wandered restlessly about the house, unable to settle to anything. Foss, sensing my mood as he always does, followed me around the house, occasionally uttering a hoarse cry, either of encouragement or (more likely) a desire for more food. I was so occupied with my thoughts squirrelling around that the ringing of the telephone startled me.

It was Roger. "Sheila? Bad news, I'm sorry. Richard Lewis was a friend of yours, wasn't he?"

"Richard? Yes, he is. . . . Did you say was? Roger, what's happened?"

"He's been found dead and I'm afraid it looks like suicide."

"Oh no!" I cried. "How awful! Where was he? At home?"

"No, he was in one of the shelters on the sea front. A woman walking her dog found him early this morning. At first they thought he was suffering from exposure—hypothermia. It was bitterly cold last night. But then they found an empty pill bottle and an empty half-bottle of whisky, so it does seem as if he took his own life. Of course we'll have to wait for the post mortem before we can be sure, but it looks pretty certain."

"Oh, poor Richard . . ."

"He was a friend of Freda Spencer, wasn't he? And didn't Rosemary tell me that there'd been some trouble between them?"

"He's been devoted to Freda for years," I said, "and she wasn't very kind to him."

"Would that be why he killed himself? I mean, now she's dead? Or is there something else? Is that what you weren't telling me the other day, Sheila?"

"Look," I said, "have you spoken to Pam?"

"No, not yet. What's that got to do with this?"

"Has anyone told her that Richard's dead?"

"No, why should they?"

"I think, when she knows—poor Pam—she'll be willing to talk to you."

"Sheila, what *is* all this?" Roger demanded.

"Go and talk to Pam, Roger, she'll explain everything."

It was late afternoon when Pam rang me. Her voice was husky with crying. "Sheila, can you come round? I'd like to talk to you. Come up to my room, it's number thirty-five."

"Of course I will. I'll come straight away."

Pam's room was a large one at the front of the hotel, overlooking the sea. She let me in and then went and stood by the window. I joined her and for a moment we neither of us said anything, but stood staring out at the lights in Wales just beginning to show in the gathering dusk across the Channel and I remembered how Richard had stood watching them in the darkness on the night of the reunion dinner.

I put my hand on Pam's shoulder. "I'm sorry," I said, "so sorry."

Her face was pale and her eyes red and puffy, but her voice was composed. "He's at peace now, thank God. But oh, Sheila, the agony he must have gone through before . . ."

"I know."

She moved over to where a tray was laid on a low table. "I told them to send up some tea," she said. "I thought we might need it. That's unless you'd rather have a drink?"

"No, tea's fine."

Her hand shook slightly when she handed me my cup, but her voice was steady as she said, "Your friend Roger told me about Richard. He's a nice young man—very kind and considerate."

"You told him everything?" I asked. "All about you and Richard and Freda?"

"Yes."

"And about where you were when Freda died?"

"Yes. I think he believes I didn't do it."

"But Richard?"

"It does seem the likeliest explanation."

"He had the greatest reason to kill Freda," I said, "and he was in such a state . . ."

"And afterwards," Pam said, "he was so odd; strange and withdrawn."

"Did he leave any sort of note?"

"The police haven't found one. They had to break into the house, you know. It seems dreadful . . ."

"So what did Roger actually say about Richard?" I asked.

"Well, he told me—you know—about him being found. And then, after I told him about Freda and what she'd done, he asked me point-blank whether I thought Richard had killed her."

"And you said?"

"That it seemed very likely that he had. Well, Richard's dead. He has no relatives to be hurt. It was simpler just to tell the truth."

I was silent for a minute, then I said, "One thing is nagging away at me. The other morning, when Roger rang to tell me about Laurence Marvell having an alibi (yes, he's in the clear), he asked me if there was anything I ought to tell him. Of course, I felt I couldn't tell him about you and Richard, but Pam, if I had and he'd gone round to see Richard, then this might not have happened. Richard might still be alive."

Pam shook her head. "But in prison," she said, "probably for the rest of his life. No, you can't wish that for him! Better the way things are."

"Yes," I said slowly, "I suppose so. It *must* have been Richard who killed her. No one else had a motive."

"Poor Richard," Pam said softly. "What a wasted life."

I looked at her. "And how about you? Are you all right?"

She smiled. "Better now I've had this talk with you. Thanks, Sheila, you've been a real friend." She picked up the teapot. "There's still some left. Would you like another cup?"

"No, I'd better get back. I must see to the supper. Michael will be back home soon."

Pam said, "I'll walk down with you."

As we passed the reception desk the girl called out, "Oh, Mrs. Watson, there's a letter for you—it came by the second post."

Pam took the letter and looked at it. "Wait a minute, Sheila," she said urgently. "It's from Richard."

She drew me over to a sofa in an alcove by the desk and opened the letter. She read it in silence and then handed it to me.

The writing was shaky and the lines were uneven and sloping downwards across the page.

> Dear Pam
>
> Do not think badly of me for choosing the coward's way out, but I could not face the future after what has happened and, of course, there can be no future for me now.
>
> Now that Freda is dead, justice has been done. I could never have forgiven her—for your sake as well as for mine.
>
> Dear Pam, put all this from your mind. Do not grieve for me because I am glad to go. Enjoy your life and be happy.
>
> God bless you.
>
> Richard

"Oh, Pam," I said. "Oh my dear!"

She was crying quietly and I felt the tears welling up in my own eyes. After a few moments she pulled herself together and said, "So that's it, then. He did do it. Well, we knew that already, but it's still a shock to read."

"I know."

"I suppose I must show it to your friend Roger. It seems a disloyal thing to do."

"I do know how you feel, Pam," I said sympathetically, "but you have to do it."

"Yes, you're right," she said, getting up. "It's got to be done. I'll go up to my room now and ring him right away."

"Will you tell your husband about Richard?" I asked.

"He knows about the baby and the abortion," she said. "But of course he always thought, as I did, that Richard had let me down. I'll be glad to put the record straight about that."

"You didn't tell him about what Freda had done that night, the night of the reunion, then?"

"No, I was too upset and confused. I just said that I wanted to stay on to be with Uncle Leslie." She smiled sadly. "I shall have a lot to tell him when I get home."

"I can imagine."

"Well, I'm off in the morning, unless the police need me to stay for anything." She gave me a hug. "Let's keep in touch, Sheila."

"Yes," I said. "Let's do that."

Later that evening I had a call from Roger.

"I gather you were with Mrs. Watson when she got the letter," he said. "I'm sorry. It must have been very upsetting for you both."

"I suppose he sent it to Pam," I said, "instead of

leaving a note at home, so that she could choose whether or not to tell you everything. He was always a thoughtful and considerate person."

"The letter certainly makes things simpler," Roger said.

"You think it clears up the murder?"

"I was actually thinking of the formalities connected with the suicide."

"But it does seem to be a sort of confession."

"I agree, but we've no actual proof that he killed Freda Spencer, no hard evidence, and the possible confession of a dead man isn't very satisfactory. There's nothing we can put up in court. I can't draw a line under the case and close the file."

"No," I said, "I suppose not. But Roger, you think Richard killed Freda, don't you?"

"Well, personally, I'm inclined to think that he did. But officially the case will have to remain on record as unsolved."

"Typical of Freda!" I said savagely. "Even her murder has to be different from everybody else's!"

Chapter Seventeen

Olive was right, the spring did come, at least the first signs of it. The shoots of the daffodils grew taller and one or two even swelled into buds, and the first iris reticulata made a brave show in the pale, late February sunshine. Inspired by all this I decided I really ought to get a little regular exercise again to shake off my winter sloth, so the following morning I went along to the Westwood. I saw a couple of heads bobbing about in the pool, though I didn't identify them, but as I was hanging up my coat in my cubicle two people came into the changing room and I heard the voices of Pauline and her special friend Maureen Philips.

I was just about to call out a greeting when I heard Pauline say, "Freda Spencer, of all people! Well, you know how Sybil's always felt about her!"

"And she'd had no idea?" Maureen asked. "For all those years? Not when Maurice was alive?"

"No, not an inkling. That's why it was such a dreadful shock, to find out like that, right out of the blue!"

I drew the curtain of my cubicle tighter shut and strained my ears.

"And there were letters, you say?"

"Yes," Pauline said, "from Freda to Maurice. That was almost the most hurtful thing, the fact that he'd kept them all that time. As I say, it was a wartime affair, when they were both in Naples, after Sybil had gone back to England in nineteen forty-four. Freda knew perfectly well that Maurice and Sybil were engaged, but she made a dead set at him and, well, you know what men are like! Of course the atmosphere was a bit hectic in Naples then, life was pretty unreal and half the Wrens were having affairs, with other people's husbands let alone fiancés. Not that I'm defending Freda—after all, Sybil was a friend, so it was a pretty low-down thing to do."

"And these letters were all in the loft?" Maureen asked.

"Yes, with a lot of wartime stuff, navigation manuals, old cap badges and a few Italian souvenirs, opera programmes and so on. Just before Christmas Sybil decided we really ought to have a good clear-out up in the loft, and she came across the box with them all in. You can imagine what it was like when she started to go through it!"

"Poor Sybil!"

"I was really worried about her, I can tell you. She was in a dreadful state! To be honest, when Freda was murdered I did wonder, just for a minute, whether Sybil might have. . . . It's a terrible thing to think about your own sister, but she was out that afternoon, said she was going for a walk—well, she often does, but still. So you can imagine how relieved I was when it turned out that it was poor Richard who killed Freda, and I can't say I blame him in the slightest, after the way that woman treated him."

The sound of the hair-drier drowned out the last of the remarks and shortly after that I heard the changing-room door closing behind them. I waited for a while until I was quite sure they were well away. I certainly didn't want Pauline to know that I had overheard her confidences.

As I swam up and down the now-deserted pool I thought about what I'd just heard. I was still more or less certain that Richard had killed Freda, but it couldn't be denied that Sybil had a motive, too. To find out that Maurice, whom she'd adored, had had an affair would have been bad enough, but that it should have been with Freda, someone she had always loathed, must have been really devastating. I do believe Sybil might be capable of murder, if the provocation was strong enough. Had her hatred of Freda been pushed beyond the limits by this chance revelation of Maurice's affair?

Revelations. First Pam and Richard, now Sybil. It was strange how the past was being thrust so brutally into the present, how the consequences of acts committed so many years ago could evoke reactions today. What we do in our youth may well come back to haunt us in our old age. Perhaps Sybil was not the only one. Who else might have suffered some injury from Freda in the past? Who else might have a motive for killing her?

I didn't tell anyone, not even Michael, what I had overheard. Partly because I was slightly guilty at having deliberately listened to what I hadn't been intended to hear, and partly because I felt that I wanted the whole business of Freda's death to be tidied neatly away so that we could all get on with our lives.

A few days later, my umbrella lowered against a gusty wind, I almost literally ran into Laurence Marvell and his friend Jimmy.

"I'm so sorry," I said, "it was silly of me to put up an umbrella on a day like this."

"Oh, Sheila, I wanted to see you," Laurence

said. "Look, do come and have a quick cup of coffee with us."

Curious to know what he wanted and quite glad to get out of the disagreeable weather, I was happy to join them in the Buttery.

"I very much wanted to see you," Laurence said, "before we go."

"Go?" I echoed.

"Yes, I've sold the cottage."

"He's coming back to London," Jimmy said, his bright, birdlike eyes scanning my face to see my reaction.

"Well," I said, "now Freda's gone I suppose there's nothing to keep you here." I noted Jimmy's smug little smile. "And, of course," I went on, "there's so much more for you in London, isn't there? Theatres, I mean, and things like that."

"Larry isn't really a *country* person," Jimmy said. "He likes the bright lights, don't you, dear?"

Laurence ignored this interjection. "Poor Freddie," he said with a sigh. "I miss her very much."

"Yes," I said, "I'm sure you do."

"It was all such a terrible shock. I really felt that Taviscombe would never be the same for me again."

"He's frightfully *sensitive,*" Jimmy confided. "He's been really *upset* about it all."

"You were lucky to find a buyer for the cottage at this time of the year," I said.

"Oh, but have you *seen* all the gorgeous things he's done to it?" Jimmy exclaimed. "It's really artistic! The lady who bought it said it was quite enchanting. Enchanting!" he repeated. "That's what she said."

"You certainly made it delightful. And you had some very nice antique pieces, I seem to remember." A Pembroke table and an oak corner cupboard, for instance. I didn't imagine for one moment that they would ever be returned to Freda's heirs and assigns.

"I've always liked nice things," Laurence said. "That was another thing that Freddie and I had in common."

"Oh, he's always had marvellous taste," Jimmy broke in. "My friend Justin—he's got this fabulous antique shop near Portobello, you should see the tourists he gets in there, Japanese, Americans, everyone—anyway, he's always said that Larry has a real eye. Oh, he's well known for it!"

"How splendid," I said, enjoying Laurence's discomfiture at Jimmy's praise. "So where will you live in London?"

"Oh, we've bought this dear little house. It's in Westbourne Grove," Jimmy said. "Practically Holland Park."

"My cousin Hilda lives in Holland Park," I said.

Jimmy looked at me with a new respect.

"I think I remember your cousin," Laurence said. "She came with you to my little tea party for poor Freddie, just after Christmas. Such a happy time."

"It's quite a small house," Jimmy said. It was plain that he didn't respond well to any mention of Freda. "*Bijou*, you might say, but it's got a lot of *potential*. I always think that's the really important thing about a house, don't you?"

I nodded gravely. "Oh, I do."

"And there's a sweet little garden at the back, very overgrown, but Larry will soon sort that, won't you, dear? He's got green fingers, you know, absolutely *green*!"

"Town gardens can be very pretty," I said.

"So you see," said Laurence, trying to take control of the conversation again, "since you were such a good friend of Freddie's I couldn't leave Taviscombe without letting you know."

"Well," I said, gathering up my things to leave, "I hope you will both be very happy in your new home."

"If you're in London, dear," Jimmy said, "do give us a tinkle. And if you ever want tickets for the ballet or the opera—I think you're a ballet person, aren't you? I thought so!—let me know. I can usually pull a few strings for a friend."

"That's very kind of you," I said. "Well, goodbye . . ."

They both got up and, to my surprise, embraced me warmly.

"Anyone," I said to Rosemary, when I was telling her all about it, "would think that we'd been the dearest of friends!"

"Oh well," she said vaguely, "you know what theatricals are like."

Her mind obviously wasn't on our conversation because we were, at that moment, attempting to deal with a minor crisis. A couple of pipes had burst at Brunswick Lodge and we were trying to clear up some of the mess in the passage by the back stairs.

"I'll just go and empty this bucket," she said, "if you can take the other one and see if you can mop up some of the water there by the stairs."

I found the mop wasn't very efficient so I resorted to trying to soak up the water with a floorcloth. I was glad of the rubber gloves I'd found in the kitchen (Freda's, I suppose) because the water was cold and quite dirty. I'd got most of it up and was just wiping the grimy tidemark the water had left behind off the front of the cupboard under the stairs, when Rosemary came back.

"Oh, that's better," she said. "Now we can get it dried out."

I got up stiffly from the crouching position I'd been obliged to adopt. "It's an odd thing about that cupboard," I said. "I thought the keyhole was all bunged up with paint, from when they did the decorating last year, but it's quite clear and it looks as if it's been opened. Did someone find the key after all?"

"I don't know. I don't think so. Matthew Paisley had that tin of keys and odds and ends he found in one of the attics . . ."

"Yes, that's right," I said. "He showed them to me. There was one very ornate one that he thought might be the one. Freda took them and said she'd give them to someone to sort out, but I can't remember who. Oh, goodness, who *was* it?"

"Well, does it matter?"

"No, I suppose not, but it's maddening not to be able to remember something."

"Oh well," Rosemary said, "we'll all be into senile decay before too long and unable to remember anything at all. Do you know, the other day neither Jack nor I could think of the word *hydrangea*! '*You* know,' we kept on saying, 'that big, blue flower!' "

"Oh yes," I agreed, "and as for remembering who was in films and plays and things . . ."

"There now." Rosemary opened the door into the garden. "We'll probably freeze, but the air should dry it out. Mr. Soames says the plumber should be here tomorrow and the water's turned off now. I really don't know why those pipes weren't properly lagged."

"Freda would have seen to it," I said.

"Yes," Rosemary agreed. "Sybil's much nicer to have around, but she isn't a patch on Freda when it comes to running things."

We looked at each other and laughed.

"That's life for you!" I said. "Come on, I think we've earned a cup of tea after all that hard manual labour."

"Good idea. And, actually, I've got a favour to ask you, which will be better asked when you're sitting down with a cup in your hand."

"Right," I said, when the tea had been made. "What is it?"

"Do you think you could *possibly* look after Delia for a couple of hours tomorrow? Jilly's got to take Alex up to Taunton to see this specialist about his foot. They're a bit worried about the way he's walking. I was going to do it myself but I broke a tooth last night and Mr. Robinson's fitted me in specially. I can meet Delia from school and take her back home—she's better in her own room with all her toys and things—if you could take over from me at about three o'clock. I hope I won't be long, but you know how behind they get in the afternoons."

"Of course I will," I said. "Delia and I get on quite well."

"Oh, bless you! It would be such a help. Actually, Roger might be back early. He's been at a conference somewhere and said he might be home by teatime."

"No, really, I'll enjoy it."

"Let's play shops. I'll be the shopkeeper and you be the person who comes in and buys things."

Trying to find a clear space, I lowered myself cautiously to the floor of Delia's room.

"All right," I said. "What have you got to sell?"

Delia indicated the collection of miniature cartons. "There's milk and there's juice and there's baked beans and there's choclit biscuits and," she picked up a carton and examined it, "chicken dinner."

"Right. I'll have a carton of milk and a chicken dinner, please."

"That's two pounds."

I scrabbled in the old handbag that Delia gave me and produced a couple of coins.

"Now you want some change," Delia announced, and gave me the two coins back again.

We played shops for quite a while, small children having an infinite capacity for repetition, and then we played schools ("I'll be the teacher and you be the children"), and then Delia wanted to thread some of the wooden beads that were scattered about, mixed up with the other toys all over the floor.

"I know," I said brightly, "let's tidy all this up and give Mummy a lovely surprise when she comes back."

Delia looked at me doubtfully, but helped me pick up a few toys.

"Shall we put them in your toy box?" I asked. I opened the lid and peered inside. "I'll just put these crayons and things into a bag so that they don't get mixed up with everything else."

As I was scrabbling about in the bottom of the toy box. I felt something metallic and pulled it out from under a couple of colouring books. It was a key. A very ornate key. A key that I knew I had seen once before.

"Delia," I said, trying to keep my voice steady, "where did you get this key?"

Delia, trying to stuff her doll's arms into a garment too small for it, looked up.

"Key?" she asked.

"Yes, darling, this key." I held it up.

Delia avoided my eye. "Don't know," she said.

"It's all right, there's nothing wrong," I said quickly. "It was very clever of you to find it. We've all been looking for it for ages."

She looked at me warily and I went on, "Daddy will be *very* pleased. Did you find it here?" She shook her head. "At Grandma's house?"

"No. I found it in the garden."

"In Grandma's garden?"

"No!" she said impatiently. "At that house, the big house where I went with Grandma."

"Brunswick Lodge?"

She nodded.

"In the garden there?"

"When I was digging."

"Of course."

"I put it in my handbag."

"Was it all muddy?" I asked.

"Yes. But," she said virtuously, "I wiped it before I put it in my bag."

I remembered Delia offering to show us what she had in her bag. There was a sound from downstairs and Roger's voice calling, "Hello? Rosemary, Delia, I'm home."

I went out onto the landing. "It's me, Sheila. Rosemary had to go to the dentist. Come up and see what your clever daughter has found."

Chapter Eighteen

When Rosemary got back, Roger and I went round to Sybil's to get a key to Brunswick Lodge.

"The cupboard under the stairs?" Sybil asked with what appeared to be genuine bewilderment. "Why on earth . . ."

"The key to it," Roger said, "Well, what *seems* to be the key, was buried in the garden."

"Well, now you've lost me!" Sybil said. "What the devil's it all about?"

While Roger was explaining I watched Sybil closely, since it now seemed that she too had had a motive for killing Freda. But she sounded honestly puzzled by the whole affair and, the more I thought about it, the less likely it was that Freda would have given the box with the keys in it to her.

It was cold in Brunswick Lodge, the stone flags of the passage adding to the general feeling of damp and chill. Roger switched on the lights, knelt down in front of the cupboard, and took out the key wrapped in a handkerchief.

"Locking the stable door after the horse has gone," he said ruefully, "since my clever daughter has wiped off any prints there might have been."

"If it had been buried in the earth," I said, "perhaps there wouldn't have been any."

"Oh well, here goes." He fitted the key in the lock and turned it. It was dark in the cupboard but Roger produced a torch and shone it inside.

"Well now," he said.

He took the handkerchief that had been wrapped round the key and, winding it round his hand, reached into the cupboard and brought out an object which he held up for me to see. It was the awl.

"It always worried me that we never found the weapon," he said.

"But what on earth is it doing here?"

"I can't imagine," Roger said, holding it up against the light bulb in the passage. "But it's definitely what killed Freda Spencer. There are traces of blood. I do believe it hasn't been wiped at all. There may even be prints."

"But why should Richard have put it in there?"

I asked. "That's supposing it was Richard who killed her. I mean, why not just throw it away?"

"Why indeed? The whole thing's a complete mystery. Tell me about the cupboard and the key again."

"For ages it was locked and no one knew where the key was. Then old Mr. Paisley found what he thought was the right one in a box of odds and ends. He gave the box to Freda just before he died—he had a stroke, I think—and she passed it on to someone to sort through and check if the key he thought was the right one did actually fit."

"And you can't remember who she passed it on to?"

"No. Isn't it ridiculous?"

"It wasn't Richard Lewis?"

"No, I'm quite sure it wasn't."

"Would he have known about it?"

"I honestly don't know."

"Were you there when she handed the box over?"

"No, someone told me. I can't remember who. I'm sorry, Roger, I'm not being much help, am I?"

"Never mind. You've done enough for one day."

"I *wish* I could remember!"

"Don't worry, it'll come back to you." He wrapped the awl carefully in the handkerchief.

"I'll just drop you back home and then I'll get this over to forensics."

"Roger," I asked, "do *you* think that Richard was the murderer?"

Roger shrugged. "In view of all this," he said, "I really don't know. You see, if he had killed Freda Spencer I'd have expected him to have left some sort of note when he committed suicide. And then, the weapon hidden away like this, and the key to the cupboard buried in the garden—it just doesn't feel right."

"No," I agreed. "It's all so, well, *convoluted*! Richard was a very straightforward sort of person, all this isn't like him at all. I suppose, after Richard killed himself, we all wanted to believe that he was the murderer—though it was so unlike him, even with the provocation he had—so that we didn't have to wonder about anyone else. It tidied things up so neatly, but of course just because things are tidy it doesn't necessarily mean that they're true."

"Well," Roger said, "as I told you before, the case is still open." He moved over to the light switch. "Come along, Sheila, we must be going. You must be chilled to the bone."

I was cold and somehow couldn't get warm, even when I got home.

"Perhaps you're sickening for something," Michael suggested helpfully.

"No, it's sort of cold inside. You know what I mean, as if your bones have turned to ice."

"Have a nice warming gin and tonic—it's a sovereign remedy against most things."

"If only," I said, "I could remember who told me about those keys! It was when I was at Brunswick Lodge, obviously, but *when*?"

"It's no good *trying* to remember," Michael said, "you'll simply drive yourself mad. If you leave it it'll just pop into your mind."

I certainly didn't feel like turning out that evening for a meeting of the Poetry Society, but I knew that Maureen Philips would be disappointed if I didn't, because she was always saying how difficult it was to get people together in the winter months.

At least this particular meeting was being held at Maureen's house, which would be relatively warm, certainly warmer than Brunswick Lodge, where we usually gathered. There was also hot coffee, liberally supplied by Brian Philips who, since he wasn't interested in poetry, spent most of the evening in the kitchen, emerging from time to time with yet another steaming jugful.

There were eight of us there, not a bad turn-out

for a winter's evening and not too many to fit into Maureen's over-furnished sitting-room. The warmth and the company helped me to relax and I found I was quite looking forward to the evening.

We'd all been asked to bring Victorian poems to read and, perhaps in a way to mourn Richard, I had chosen part of Tennyson's *In Memoriam*:

> He is not here; but far away
> The noise of life begins again,
> And ghastly thro' the drizzling rain
> On the bald street breaks the blank day.

I felt my voice crack and was glad to sit down again. Maurice Williams, who always has to be different, embarked on an interminable poem by a long (and justifiably) forgotten poet that none of us had ever heard of. The verse—it couldn't be dignified by the name of poetry—had a soporific quality and I found myself almost drifting into sleep, when a couple of lines impinged on my consciousness.

> Fly with me, then, immortal bard
> To fair Parnassus, olive-crowned . . .

I gave an involuntary exclamation that made Maureen, who was sitting opposite, look at me in alarm. I hastily turned it into a cough and tried to compose myself, waiting impatiently for the evening to be over so that I could telephone Roger.

"Roger, it's Sheila. Look, I'm sorry to be ringing you so late!"

"No, that's fine. I was going to call you in the morning, anyway. I've got some news."

"What is it?"

"I've heard from forensics," Roger said. "That awl *did* have fingerprints on it. So now I have to take the prints of everyone who might have been in Brunswick Lodge . . ."

"You may not need to do that. I've remembered who Freda gave those keys to. It was Olive Clark."

"Olive Clark?"

"Yes."

"You think Olive Clark might have killed her cousin?"

"I know it seems unlikely. She's not the sort of person you think of in connection with a murder."

"Quite the wrong type, I would have said. Anyway, I thought she was devoted to her cousin."

"Freda always kept her in tow," I said, "but Olive was very concerned about Emily—you know, she's absolutely devoted to her—and," I added, my voice rising with excitement, "if Freda told her that she was cutting Emily out of her will in favour of Laurence Marvell . . ."

"It's a possibility, I suppose."

"The only trouble is, though, she has an alibi. Pam Nelson saw her at West Lodge that afternoon."

"Ah." Then, after a pause, "Did she say what time in the afternoon she saw her?" Roger asked.

"Well, no, now you come to mention it, she didn't."

"I shall have to go and see Miss Clark tomorrow."

"Yes, I suppose you'll have to. About the keys, at any rate."

We were both silent for a moment.

"She's a bit peculiar nowadays," I said.

"In what way peculiar?"

"Most of the time she's her old self, but then she suddenly starts talking about God."

"Oh."

"Roger, do you think I could come with you when you go and see Olive? Partly because of her being peculiar, and partly because it might help for her to see a face she knows."

"Well, it's not exactly according to the rule book—but, as you say, it might help. All right, then, I'll call for you tomorrow at about ten o'clock and we'll go round there together."

"Sheila, dear, what a lovely surprise!"

"Hello, Olive. Sorry to drop in like this. I've brought Roger to see you."

"Come in, both of you." She ushered us into the sitting-room, where Tinker was lying stretched out in front of the gas fire. I stooped to stroke him and Olive said, "I don't usually light this fire until later on, but he sat down in front of it until I put it on. Who's a clever boy!"

"Olive," I said as we all sat down, "Roger would like to have a word with you."

"Yes dear, of course." She turned to him and smiled. "Now you're Jilly's husband, aren't you? And you have those two dear little children . . ."

"Roger's a police officer," I broke in.

"Yes, dear, I did know. Rosemary was telling me what dreadfully long hours you have to work. It does seem such a shame."

I tried again. "Roger wants to ask you about the key to the cupboard under the stairs at Brunswick Lodge," I said. "You had that tin with the keys in it that Matthew Paisley found, didn't you?"

"Yes, dear. And, do you know, the key he said was the right one *did* fit."

I looked appealingly at Roger.

"Miss Clark," he said, "did you put the awl from the Museum Room in that cupboard?"

"Yes, that's right."

"And," he paused, "did you know that the awl had been used to kill Freda Spencer?"

"Well, of course I did."

"Miss Clark, did you kill Freda Spencer?"

Olive looked bewildered. "Freda's dead," she said.

"Yes, Miss Clark, we know that. Did you kill her?"

She leaned forward and spoke confidentially to me. "Do you know what Freda was going to do? She was going to leave all her money and the house and everything to that man! Nothing for Emily, nothing at all. Now that was wrong. Wasn't it wrong?"

"Yes," I said, "I think it was."

"And unjust, too. Justice is mine, saith the Lord."

"Olive," I said gently, "did you kill Freda?"

"It was the will of the Lord," she said simply.

Roger began to caution her but she ignored him and continued to address me. " 'Let the little children come unto Me,' that's what He said. He wouldn't let Emily's children be cheated of their birthright, would He? Not those innocent little children. You see," she said earnestly, "when Freda nearly died, when it happened twice, then I knew what He wanted me to do." She nodded. "It was a sign, you see."

"Yes," I said, "I see. Can you tell us what happened? Roger has to know."

Olive sat back in her chair, a far away look in her eyes. "Freda was always an unkind girl. Do you know, when we were young she did something really terrible."

I glanced at Roger and he nodded imperceptibly.

"What did she do?" I asked.

"Papa was very strict," Olive said, "and although I longed for a pet animal he would never allow it. One day I found a dear little cat, a stray, in the garden. I hid it in one of the sheds, the old tool shed where no one ever went. I took food from the house for her and—oh, it was wonderful—she had three lovely kittens."

She looked at me and I smiled encouragingly.

"Somehow or other Freda found out about them. At first she was interested and helped me to find food and look after them. Then she got bored, I suppose, and cross because they were *my* secret and not hers. She always said she never told Papa, but I know she did, because no one else knew about them and, anyway, she could never bear anyone to have something she didn't have. The little cat was taken away and the kittens—the kittens were drowned . . ." She broke off and tears ran down her face.

I went and sat beside her on the sofa and took her hand.

"I think about it so often," she said. "It's as if it happened yesterday. I will never forgive her."

"Olive," I said, "what happened at Brunswick Lodge on that Sunday afternoon?"

"That afternoon?"

"When Freda—died."

"She asked me to go and help her with sorting out the programmes for the concert," Olive said with a momentary return to her old manner. "That's when she told me . . ."

"About leaving Laurence the money? So you killed her with the awl?"

"The Lord guided my hand."

"But why," Roger asked, "did you put the awl in that cupboard?"

"I had the key in my bag. I'd meant to give it to Freda."

"But why not just throw it away?"

Olive looked shocked. "Oh, I couldn't have

done that! It's a very important artefact. Freda said so."

"And you buried the key in the garden?"

"Well," Olive said in a matter-of-fact voice, "I knew someone would find it when they dug the garden in the spring, when all the fuss had died down and Freda had been forgotten."

Roger and I exchanged glances.

"So, after that, what did you do?"

"Well," she said briskly, "I suddenly remembered I'd promised to go and read to old Mr. Benson at West Lodge. His sight's very bad now, you know. He was expecting me at three and I'm afraid I was a bit late. Poor old soul, he thought I'd forgotten him!"

"Miss Clark," Roger said, "did anyone else know that you'd killed Freda? Emily, for instance? Did you tell her?"

Olive looked puzzled. "Why should I tell her?" she asked. "God moves in a mysterious way."

I remembered now how she had used that phrase after the funeral.

"So she didn't know," Roger persisted.

"God may reveal it to her one day," Olive said. "He may speak to her as He spoke to me. Thy will be done. That's what we pray for, isn't it?" She smiled at me, her old, sweet smile.

"Miss Clark," Roger said gently, "I want you to

come down to the police station with me and make a statement, so that someone can write down what you've just told us."

"A statement?"

"It has to be written down," I said.

"All right, dear, if you say so. I'll just go and put on my coat and hat."

When she had gone out of the room, I said to Roger, "I still can't believe it—Olive killing someone!"

"She's obviously extremely attached to her niece," he said. "And, of course, she's mentally disturbed."

"Why did no one notice she was becoming so odd?"

"She's old, she was emotionally upset and confused."

"Actually," I said, "all this religious business, I think it's probably come on since the murder. I believe she killed Freda because she was so dreadfully upset about Emily not getting the money, but then she somehow had to justify what she'd done."

"You're probably right," Roger said. "It would obviously be easier for her to feel that she was God's instrument, that she was only doing God's will, rather than admit to herself that she was a murderer. She was obviously in a pretty fragile mental state before; this simply pushed her over the edge."

"Poor Olive."

"I think, perhaps, I'd better get her vicar down to the station."

"Mr. Whipple. Yes, that's a good idea."

"There'll have to be a doctor there too, of course." He sighed. "I hate this sort of thing."

"Roger, what will happen to her?"

"As I said, there'll be a doctor—two doctors, actually. She'll be sectioned, I expect. You'd better get in touch with her niece. Is she the only relative?"

"Yes, there's no one else. Oh, Roger, it's so terribly *sad*!"

Olive came back into the room. "There we are, then, all ready. Oh, Sheila, could you do something for me, dear? Tinker hasn't had his elevenses yet. Could you give him some? There's a tin open in the kitchen."

"Yes," I said, "of course I will."

"And give my love to Michael, won't you, dear? Tell him we'll go to Bridgwater Carnival next year."

"Yes," I said, "I'll tell him."

When the front door had closed behind them, I went into the kitchen, with Tinker following at my heels. His dish was on the draining board and

I emptied the rest of the food from the tin into it. Tinker gave a faint, expectant cry and I put the dish down for him.

"There you are," I said. "Poor Tinker, poor old boy."

Tinker didn't raise his eyes from his dish but went on eating.

"Don't worry," I said, my eyes suddenly full of tears, "don't worry, we'll look after you."

Then I went out into the hall to telephone Emily.